Slavonic Dances

Reviews of Tom Hubbard's Previous Novels

Marie B. (Ravenscraig Press, 2008):

'I loved this book, not least because of all that it did not say. The spaces and silences are as eloquent as the writing.' Catherine Czerkawska, *Edinburgh Review*.

'Thanks to Ravenscraig Press for Tom Hubbard's *Marie B.* [...] recapturing the young Russian painter Marie Bashkirtseff and the world of French realism, often rendered in a braid Scots which seems absolutely right, for she could have been a "Glasgow Girl" alongside Crawhall and Lavery.'

Christopher Harvie, *Sunday Herald*.

The Lucky Charm of Major Bessop (Grace Note, 2014):

Subtitled 'a grotesque mystery of Fife'. 'Draws you in and keeps you guessing, right to the end'. Morelle Smith,

Textualities (online).

'Tom Hubbard is a remarkable Scottish author [...] a rare example of a Scottish man of letters [...] his intriguingly quirky second novel [...] Hubbard's Fife is perhaps a poet's one – a Fife of bloody medieval ballads, outside of time, its landscape blanketed at any moment by mirky mist and haar'. Andrew Hook, *Scottish Review* (online).

'A strange novel of misadventure and mystery, set in a hinterland of the imagination [...] a place just beyond reality, a psychological terrain'. *Scottish Books* (online).

Slavonic Dances

Three novellas:
Mrs Makarowski – The Kilt
– The Carrying Stream

Tom Hubbard

GRACE NOTE PUBLICATIONS

Slavonic Dances
This edition published 2017 by
Grace Note Publications C.I.C.
Grange of Locherlour,
Ochtertyre, PH7 4JS,
Scotland

books@gracenotereading.co.uk
www.gracenotepublications.co.uk

ISBN 978-1-907676-89-5

First published in 2017

In Memoriam
RONALD STEVENSON
1928-2015

CONTENTS

PREFACE

Tom Hubbard and I first met ten years ago on a bus going out of Edinburgh. We were on our way to West Linton, to meet our mutual friends, the late Ronald Stevenson (composer, pianist, teacher, author, and comrade-in-arts to hundreds, in five continents) and Marjorie Stevenson (archivist, community nurse, and similarly a great comrade-in-arts). There, in this Den of Musiquity, from which so much beauty and kindness had poured over the decades, as it still does, we shared a feast of conversation, not to mention food and drink. We ranged over so many topics I cannot remember them all, but what sticks in my mind is the way we were able, in that Bunyanesque Interpreter's House, to establish in an instant what Ronald called 'enharmonic relationships', that is to say the human equivalents of (for example) the note A flat being the same as G sharp; but, as Ronald explained from his piano stool, this enharmony only works in a company that is of 'equal temperament'. (That piano stool, by the way, had once been Ferruccio Busoni's; but that is another story, one that contains multitudes.)

I mention this meeting and this musical metaphor because they sum up what has been a constant in Tom's life: a rich counterpoint of friendships and sharings. As a wandering scholar, working as a teacher and researcher in a dozen countries, Tom has been able to map out a view of the world according to a sort of cultural triangulation. He sees his native Fife, and Scotland, from different perspectives, at the same time making his home, and being at home, in places that may be 'abroad', but are never foreign.

Polyglot and polymath, and a latter-day goliard, Tom has been waiting all his life to write this latest book, *Slavonic Dances*; or, to be more accurate, this book has been waiting all Tom's life to get itself written. It is crammed with the fruits of his travels, and, as you might expect, it shows a practised literary craft, making it a delight to read, and to dance along with. If *Slavonic Dances* was a musical composition, which I think it wants to be, it would be a three-movement symphony. What is more, in a Wagnerian way, but more briefly and lightly, it is 'through-composed', with certain leitmotifs threading from 'Mrs Makarowski' (with its Polish focus), through 'The Kilt' (with a Czechoslovakian focus), to 'The Carrying Stream' (where Scotland and Russia are shown in conjunction, as astronomers say of planets).

When Tom and I last met, in a diner on Glasgow's Byres Road, how we wished that Ronald and Marjorie could be with us as we looked over the proofs of Tom's triple-decker on his laptop. How we wished that we could discuss with them such things as Tom's references to music in 'The Carrying Stream', in particular Chaliapin's singing of the title role in

Mussorgsky's opera *Boris Godunov*, and the continuing need in Europe's present dark turmoil for his Holy Fool, or *yurodivy*. (Tom's character Davie Ure, in 'Mrs Makarowski', implies that that is the case.)

When you read this lovely, many-voiced book, travelling with it across borders and back through generations, you will find that you enter into a very various company; and, as you proceed, you will easily braid Tom's cast of characters with associations of your own.

John Berger has described language, in particular the printed, published page, in terms of place: it is 'an assembly point', where the dead and the living meet, and strangers and friends, from near and far. That convivial description fits *Slavonic Dances* perfectly.

David Betteridge
Glasgow, November, 2016

David Betteridge is a retired teacher and teacher-trainer. With the designer Tom Malone he has produced ten poetry pamphlets under the aegis of Rhizome Press. His most recent book is a collection of socialist poems, with drawings by Bob Starrett, called *Slave Songs and Symphonies* (Culture Matters/Manifesto Press, 2016).

AUTHOR'S NOTE

I'm indebted to a number of publications which I consulted for the purposes of research and brief quotation. I used the editions which came most readily to hand in my own library.

For 'Mrs Makarowski' I found these books to be helpful: Diane M. Henderson, ed., *The Lion and the Eagle: Reminiscences of Polish Second World War Veterans in Scotland* (Cualann Press, 2001); T.M Devine and David Hesse, eds., *Scotland and Poland: Historical Encounters, 1500-2010* (John Donald [Birlinn], 2011.) Joseph Conrad's 'Prince Roman', which is quoted in the novella, appears in his *Tales of Hearsay and Last Essays* (Penguin, 1944).

Indispensable to 'The Kilt' were Zdeněk Mlynář, *Nightfrost in Prague: The End of Humane Socialism* (Hurst, 1980); David Caute, *Sixty-Eight: The Year of Barricades* (Paladin, 1988); Mark Kurlansky, *1968: The Year that Rocked the World* (Vintage, 2005).

'The Carrying Stream' draws on my reading of M.D. Calvocoressi, *Mussorgsky* (Dent, 1946) and Harold C. Schonberg, *The Lives of the Great Composers*, volume 2 (Futura, 1975). Quotations of Scottish poets are from Tom Scott, *The Collected Shorter Poems* (Agenda / Chapman Publications, 1993); *Perviligium Scotiae (Scotland's Vigil): Tom Scott, Somhairle MacGill-Eain,*

Hamish Henderson (Etruscan Books, 1997); *The Complete Poems of Hugh MacDiarmid*, 2 volumes (Martin Brian & O'Keeffe, 1978); George Bruce, *Landscapes and Figures* (Akros, 1967). The two quatrains beginning 'The blae o the lift' are actually by me: this poem as titled 'Lyric on a Theme o Ernesto Cardenal' first appeared in *Poetry Ireland Review*, No. 31 (1991), and subsequently in Tom Hubbard, ed., *The New Makars* (Mercat Press, 1991) and in my pamphlet *Scottish Faust* (Kettillonia, 2004). It has been translated into Gaelic, Polish and Spanish.

MRS MAKAROWSKI

Krakowiak

1

The old man's hand shook as he raised the biscuit to his mouth. Crumbs fell on his chest; he persisted in the chewing.

His wife wiped his lips.

The younger woman had suggested that this time she bring a lighter cup for his tea, and the old man's wife had agreed.

'He'll no gie in easy, hen,' remarked the old lady. 'He never did.'

'Ah'll leave ye be then, Ina. Juist let me ken if ye need me, Ah'm no far awa.'

Some ten minutes later the girl returned, and with a nurse. The old man was given something to calm him down; Ina was told that he'd soon doze off, though she was already aware of the drug's effects.

'That's a pity, hen,' sighed Ina. 'Ah wis juist hopin fir a wee bit time wi him whiles he wis awake.'

The young woman had been alerted, not by Ina, accustomed as that lady was to the old man's ways, but by his sudden shouting, and the inevitable commotion this caused in the adjacent TV lounge.

'It wis yesterday, hen,' explained the girl. 'The first time he shout … said it. We couldnae mak it oot – something like, "dry it, sir"?

'Ah ken whit he means.' The old lady lowered her gaze. 'Ah ken it ower weill.'

'It upsets him, whitever it is.'

'Ah couldnae explain it ti ye, hen. Even wi him drappin aff. Ah'd be feart he'd still hear me and that wad mak maitters worse.'

'I understaund,' said the girl, though she didn't; in any case, it was time to change the subject. 'When dae ye think Davie'll be up?'

'He said he'd cry in the morn, hen. He had ti be at the uni the-day.'

'A guid man, yer Davie. He cares. We'll hae yer man spic-and-span fir him, Ina.' The girl instantly regretted the remark: the old guy wasn't spic-and-span at the moment. Ina said nothing, gave the girl a hug, then left the home, for home.

2

If an inter-school rugger match at Crockarkie College was a big day in the calendar of that institution, the always-expected appearance of Sir Andrew and Lady Marion Bruntsfield was even more sensational. Especially as regards the good Lady. It was a necessarily private joke, among those teachers and pupils who were less than reverential, that her entry ought to be marked by the school ensemble playing 'The Arrival of the Queen of Sheba'.

As one of the teachers put it, *sotto voce*, even Solomon in all his glory was not arrayed like Sir Andrew. The bewhiskered rubicundity of his face was topped by a deerstalker, adorned with a feather, and which hid his baldness. Pristine waistcoat – which he pronounced weskit; bespoke tweed suit; plus fours. Many had told him that he'd look spiffing in a kilt (to which he was entitled through his Highland clan line) but he'd declare that though 'I've got the arse for it, it's no-can-do in the old legs department.'

Then, from the subtlest folds of his attire, he'd produce the flask containing his emphatically stronger loyalty to Highland tradition. His lady would look on with a pinched expression: *he could wipe his own lips.*

Down the brae from the main gate and North Lodge, the phenomenal pair arrived in a vehicle to which all teachers and pupils could find it in themselves to be not only reverential, but envious. 'Leave the old shootin'-brake at the castle,' Sir Andrew would ponder to himself and anyone else within earshot, 'but a special occasion requires the Jag!' Lady Bruntsfield had been heard to remark, on more than one occasion, that she'd rather arrive, on 'special occasions', in a coach-and-horses.

She was tall, taller it seemed than her husband, who was in fact of the same height: his girth explained the illusion. For she was slender, and she claimed the elegance which should go with that. The face suggested determination as well as hazardous charm: the perfectly-jawed smile told you that she might get to like you, as long as you knew your place. The high cheekbones tempered her Englishness with a hint of the exotic, and atop the arrangement of short dark hair there presided a wide-brimmed hat with a floral display whose polychromatism set off the blackness of the hat, her necklace, her dress, her stockings, and her shoes. There had been comments on her old-fashioned, old-world appearance, Victorian-Edwardian ('got up to the nines,' as Sir Andrew would comment), which co-existed oddly with her perceived status as a free spirit in her mid-to-late thirties and living in the mid-to-late nineteen-sixties.

The teachers and pupils of Crockarkie, then, lightly mocked her – and intensely desired her.

Crockarkie won the match; its captain was Sir Andrew's nephew, so the couple were endowed with congratulations, handshakes, and – from a few emboldened fathers of team members – slaps on the back (for Sir Andrew) and certain lingering embraces (for Lady Marion). Mothers, too awed to attempt familiarity, curtseyed, and thus felt able to report, long after, that they 'had met a baronetess'. That lady, freeing herself on glimpsing a robust young man heading in her direction, ran lightly towards him, took his arm, and informed him that he was terrific.

His uncle, Sir Andrew, agreed that he was indeed terrific. 'Yes, Rab,' smiled his aunt. 'Your parents could have been proud of you, had they been here.' Rab's branch of the Bruntsfields was 'out East' and rarely showed up on its native island.

'Grub, Mari, old girl,' breathed Sir Andrew. 'Let's get away from these ghastly people and pounce on the grub.'

Overseeing the 'grub' at a series of tables was a small middle-aged woman of open countenance. 'Careful wi thon, hen,' she warned one of her subordinates. 'Hit's heavy, Ah'm no wantin ye daein yersel a mischief.'

A portly figure hobbled up.

'Hello, Sir Andrew,' smiled the small woman. 'Ye're the first the-day. The ithers arenae hungry yit.'

'Oh, they will be, Mrs Mac,' said the baronet. 'I'm just gettin' my retaliation in first, as they say.'

Sir Andrew liked to declare that he didn't stand on ceremony. From his childhood on the estate, he had always befriended its workforce; from his adolescence, he had realised that these 'chaps', and even more the 'chapesses', could teach him a thing or two about the real world. He pleaded with 'Mrs Mac' that she call him not Sir Andrew, but Sir Andy, or better still Andy. She'd have been a damn fine woman in her time, Mrs Mac; lucky man, whoever had her. Probably not much older than Marion, but Mrs Mac's type shows wear and tear early: sad business. Now she looked of an age when, on both sides, pleasantries would suffice. Come to think of it, he himself was 'of an age', and didn't just look it. Bugger.

Lady Bruntsfield approached the tables and instructed a member of Mrs Mac's staff to supply her with a slice of gâteau and a glass of red wine.

'Who is that person you were talking to, Andrew?'

'Oh, her, Mari? It's Mrs Mac – can't quite remember the rest of her name – ah yes, MacCarrawskie, something like that. Funny name, hadn't come across it before.' He turned to the small woman. 'Mrs Mac – my wife, Lady Bruntsfield.'

Mrs Mac, preoccupied with lifting an urn, was unable to curtsey; Lady Bruntsfield inclined her head slightly: more of a nod than a bow.

Parents, boys, and college staff were approaching the tables.

'Sod it,' said Lady Bruntsfield. 'The hordes are descending. Let's get out of here. What did you say that woman's name was?'

'MacCarriskie – MacCarrawskie. Sounds like the name of a good malt, ha ha!'

'Yes, you must try it some time – darling.' Lady Bruntsfield lingered on that last word.

'Nice woman,' said Sir Andrew with some emphasis. 'Salt of the earth.'

'I daresay. But her name – '

'Oh yes, Mari, have you come across it before?'

'It's not a Scottish name. It's Polish – Makarowski.'

'By thunder! You don't say?'

Lady Bruntsfield stared at her husband. 'I should know, shouldn't I?'

'Ah yes, Mari – of course … you would. So should I – these fellows were billeted up at Largo House. Brave chaps. The war effort couldn't have been the same without 'em. Got to know one or two. Liked their drink. As did I, ha ha! Could never pronounce their names, though – don't blame the drink for that.'

The festivities at Crockarkie came to an end. 'They huvnae left us aa that muckle,' said Mrs Makarowski to her assistants, 'the gannets! Still, thae young lawdies deserved it. Nou, youse yins, tak whit's left hame wi ye, it'll no dae yer menfolk and yer bairns fir their supper, but it'll help!' The young girls and women in her charge shared her laughter. 'And mind thae Crockarkie

9

lawdies! Cooped up in thon big hoose … onythin could happen!' They laughed all the more.

Seated in the Jag, Sir Andrew advised his wife: 'Now don't be thinking of Mrs Mac as a little woman from the village. More a wee wifie frae the toun, ha ha!'

Despite his accent, Sir Andrew considered himself a patriotic Scot. Lady Bruntsfield sniffed.

'I'll bear that in mind – darling.'

3

Normally, Mrs Ina Makarowski, *née* McCloskey, had little contact with the boys of Crockarkie College. She regretted that, as she was fond of children. She had none of her own – except for her nephew, Davie Ure. Davie was her sister's son, and she had found herself increasingly responsible for him since his mother's health began to deteriorate.

At Crockarkie Mrs Makarowski was responsible for the running of the school kitchen; that was her place of work except when outdoor catering was required, during the summer, for sports and parents' days. Apart from these occasions, the only time when the boys saw her and her staff was when these ladies were lined up in the dining-hall at the conclusion of the Christmas dinner. Each year, following the applause, she would use the same form of address:

'Thank ye very much boys, and we hope ye have a nice holiday.'

Over these next few weeks she was able to devote herself to one child, Davie Ure.

She used to wonder whom, in her family, Davie 'took efter'. He was an 'awfy quiet lawdie, wi his neb aye in a book.'

Davie was close to his uncle, Władysław Makarowski, or 'Vwaddie' as his wife would call him. The Silesian coal miner turned war veteran turned Fife coal miner told the boy about the homeland to which he would never make a permanent return, apart from the family visits which had become more possible. He taught his mother-tongue to Davie, who was a quick student.

'See thaim when they're babblin awa ti each ither,' Mrs Makarowski would tell her friends. 'Hit's mebbe juist as weill Ah cannae understaund a word, as Ah wouldnae want ti ken whit they're sayin aboot me!'

Vwaddie was also the name by which her husband was known to his workmates – specifically 'Vwaddie the Pole'. He didn't say much to them, not on account of his command of English, or rather Scots, which over the years had become excellent, but because of his temperament. He was considered 'friendly enough, likes, but awfy dour' – a curious observation, coming from a body of men notorious for their economy of expression.

'The laddie's like Vwaddie,' smiled one of Mrs Makarowski's friends with a gift for daft rhyming. Yet Vwaddie wasn't always 'like' the withdrawn child Davie, and certainly not when the handsome, uniformed foreigner met the young Ina in a Leven dance-hall some twenty years earlier, back in the 1940s. He tried to teach her the *krakowiak*: the laughability of the results served to draw closer together the Scottish girl and the Polish soldier.

At their wedding the daft rhymer observed that Ina didn't need to change her surname by much: from McCloskey to Makarowski was surely the shortest step imaginable. It wasn't until sometime after the Poznań rising and Gomułka's return to power in 1956 that Vwaddie felt able to visit what remained of his family in Poland. His wife accompanied him, and found herself with a further change of name, from Ina to Ajna, and was addressed as Pani Makarowska. She stared everywhere – it was her first visit to another country – and couldn't hold back her tears at the condition of its people. After a meal with her husband's surviving relatives in a small village near Katowice, she suffered severe stomach pains; she had been the only one to decline the vodka, which had offset the effects of dubious sausages on the insides of her Polish in-laws.

By 1967 Ina was out of work. Crockarkie College had been a 'clean' reincarnation of the scandal-ridden Mauletoun School; that is to say, Crockarkie occupied the same 'Big Hoose', in north-east Fife, that had been host to Mauletoun; 'the place,' Lady Marion Bruntsfield would observe to her husband's nephew, 'had seen better days, when it was home to one of the noblest families in the land.' Crockarkie had retained one or two of the undisgraced members of Mauletoun's teaching staff, but the taint of former associations proved to be overwhelming. The college governors decided that it was too late to consider further reforms such as the admission of girls. Ina Makarowski's loss was also, if in another sense, that of Lady Marion, as she was deprived of yet another site where she could play the *grande dame*. Moreover, as her husband would remark, in an effort to humour her, 'Never mind, you *are* getting on a bit, old gel.'

Yet Ina's catering skills, which included her reputation for training and retaining staff, enabled her to land her 'dream job' in the kitchen of the Balmurdie House Hotel, a little beyond her home town of Leven and just off the main road to St Andrews. During the summer of 1971, Sir Andrew Bruntsfield's regimental staff dinner took place at Balmurdie: he and his old comrades were accompanied by their wives. Lady Marion felt isolated and bored: what was the point of social climbing, she had concluded, if you were climbing into this. Her attempts to converse with the other ladies, whom she found terribly common, increased her irritation, and she was reduced to asking one of them to pass the bottle, which she kept within her reach for the remainder of the meal.

And a jolly good feast it was too, she said to herself. Pity about the company. Sod it, I'm going off to the kitchen to thank cook. Clearly nobody else is going to do that. Why not me?

Sir Andrew was aghast as she pulled back her chair and attempted, on unobligingly high heels, to march out of the dining hall. 'Steady on, old gel!' Waiters parted before her as she approached the kitchen, pushed the swing doors, and faced a startled Ina Makarowski.

Ina recognised Marion before Marion recognised Ina, who mentioned their previous encounter at Crockarkie.

'Of course…' gasped Lady Bruntsfield. 'I'm afraid I was rather rude …'

No, no, protested Ina.

'But I must thank you for …' The lady stumbled; Ina reached out a hand.

'Thank you, thank you.' Ina saw tears on Marion's cheeks. 'Can Ah help ye, yer leddyship?' 'No, no, it's nothing … I …'

Ina was confused. She stared at the lady. She must get back to work, and excused herself.

'Yes … quite so… I wish you well, Mrs Mac. You … and your husband. A gallant man, I'm sure …'

Wiping her eyes with a napkin offered by Ina, Lady Marion Bruntsfield returned erratically to the dining hall, her fellow-guests, and a perspiring Sir Andrew.

4

Ina didn't know what to do about young Davie, but did it anyway, and it seemed to work.

'Gets inti a wee corner by his-sel,' she'd tell friends and co-workers, 'and wullnae speak. Ye hae ti coax it oot o him. But he comes roond. Vwaddie and me, we've got oor different weys o daein it. Ah gie him a cuddle, puir lawdie, and Vwaddie, he talks ti him, deil Ah ken whit aboot.

'He's a clever lawdie, though, nae doobt aboot thon. There never ony problem aboot whit ti buy him fir his birthday or Christmas – aye a book token. That's best, shairly. I wadnae ken whit book he'd want, he'd mebbe hae it aareadies.'

They'd ask Ina, 'Has he no got a girlfriend yit?' 'Is he no winchin?' Bolder ones would ask, 'He's aa richt that wey, is he?'

Ina would stare, then: 'Deed ay. He's juist bydin his time. He's mairrit on his books!' She'd laugh, as if trying not to sigh.

Truly Davie was a bit of a problem. Try as Ina could to feed him well (and she knew a lot about feeding folk well), he grew gangly, and seemed to be nonplussed, every time he was seated, about where to position his arms and legs.

He would bump into furniture and other physical objects that were an obstacle to no-one but himself.

Ina was anxious for him to have his eyes tested, but the opticians told her that it was unnecessary for him to have so many appointments as frequently as she wished. His myopia was severe, no doubt about that, but his sight alone couldn't explain his condition. Doctors and psychologists came up with diagnoses that baffled Ina.

'He's young, Mrs Makarowski,' said one, 'but his wits will see him through.' One of her friends observed that Davie 'had an awfy imagination', and yet another remarked (privately) that 'he'd mebbe mak TV shows and films, though ye couldnae see him starrin in ony o them.'

'Ay', thought Ina, 'they're mebbe richt. There's something aboot him.' Davie was always top of his class; he'd surely get into university. That offered reassurance to her. And yet …

Two years after her second encounter with Marion Bruntsfield, Ina experienced a third. They recognised each other in the Ladies' at the Balmurdie House Hotel.

'Yer leddyship,' exclaimed Ina. 'Ye're back.'

'Yes, I'm back. And so are you. But you look divine.' Marion was grinning.

'Oh … ay… I dinnae work here ony mair. It's my leavin pairty, in thon room ower there.' She indicated the part of the hotel that was considerably 'less graund' than the dining hall from which Marion had emerged.

'The meal was awfully good again, Mrs Ma... let me call you Ina; you must have passed on your magic.'

'Ay, the lassies'll be jynin us efter they're finished. I wondered if you'd be here – we kent Sir Andrew wis haein anither –'

Lady Bruntsfield darkened. 'Yes, and it was worse than ever, no, no, not the food ... oh bugger I must be getting back. Awfully good to see you again ... Ina ... and I'm sorry if I ever upset you.'

An hour later Marion departed the suite adjoining the dining hall, attempting a dignified stride. Hazily she sought out the other wing of the mansion, found the site of Ina's party, and tottered on her heels as she waited for a chance to catch the attention of her new friend.

'Yer leddysh ...'

'Marion, Marion, please, lemme sit ... thank you, young man.' Davie had vacated his chair and offered it to the lady. 'Ina, Ina ... I'm frightfully pissed. Bloody Rab ... Rab ... Andy's nev-yoo ... ignored me. 'S not a gennleman. Andy should've told him. Rab ... Rab ... sitting there, pawing some tart or other ...'

Ina sat, staring, then leaned forward as the younger woman swayed perilously in her direction. Marion liberally deployed the f-word in all its senses and none, as Ina thought to herself, *Leddy? ... she's nae leddy ... language like thon ...*

But the wumman's no richt, she's needin help.

'Dinnae fash, hen.' Ina took her by the hand. Marion didn't understand a word but the gesture was clear.

'Leddy ... weill, Marion. This is Davie.'

'Your son?'

'My nephew, hen.'

'Oh yes. How nice.' Marion glanced at the young fellow, then turned her attention to the other man with Ina. He was in his early fifties; seemed startled by Marion's appearance; said nothing.

'Mr Makarowski, I believe?'

Mr Makarowski nodded in reply.

'I am also Polish.'

Mr Makarowski was again startled.

'On my mother's side,' continued Lady Bruntsfield. 'My ancestors were Polish cavalrymen, and my grandfather and great-uncles, they all served.'

His voice not much above a whisper, Mr Makarowski asked her for names.

'The family name was Szanc.'

Mr Makarowski passed from startled to astonished.

'Szanc.' He uttered the name with quiet deliberation. 'Szanc.'

Lady Bruntsfield let out a nervous giggle. 'Yes, a name I could pronounce.' Mr Makarowski did not respond to that, but the lady felt impelled towards loquacity. 'I'm afraid I'm not terribly good with foreign names. My husband, he's the most incredible idiot, but he tells me that I have the accent to match my cheekbones, all pukka and so refined, isn't that awfully funny …'

'Szanc,' repeated Władysław Makarowski. 'It was name of my commanding officer. Józef Szanc. I thought he was good man.'

'That's him. One of my great-uncles. Bit of a black sheep, actually, according to my mother, but she didn't say more.'

'He disappeared during war. We did not know what happened to him. It was sudden. Perhaps they killed him.'

'The Germans?'

'Perhaps. It was big loss to us. Very big loss.'

Lady Bruntsfield leaned forward and touched his arm. He did not observe the gesture. 'No doubt he was a hero,' declared the lady. 'I'm sure he was a gallant man, like yourself.'

'I hope.'

During these exchanges, Lady Bruntsfield sobered up somewhat, but there was now an awkward pause. It was the cue for Ina, who had remained silent and nonplussed during the conversation between the strange posh woman and her husband.

'That's awfy nice, Leddy … Marion, then. Yez have got something in common, you two. Why no come and visit us sometime … Marion?' She wrote their address for the lady, who did not reciprocate, but who

19

remarked that she was delighted to make new friends, and so unexpectedly.

Ina thought: *I juist hope she minds her language in front o the lawdie.*

'Ach, here, we're leavin Davie oot o the conversation. Davie, son, can ye no say somethin ti the leddy? Tell her aboot yer studyin?' She smiled at Marion. 'He's a braw lawdie, but he's awfy shy.'

Ina went on to tell Marion about Davie's success at college, the prizes he was winning …

'I'm afraid,' confessed Marion, 'that I was always a bit of a thicko. My governess could do nothing for me. To tell the truth, I was terribly spoiled, didn't see any need to work hard, I could just ride ponies, marry well …' She said no more, and for the first time took in the presence of Davie Ure.

One wouldn't, she thought to herself, *want him anywhere near one's best porcelain.*

5

Whit a braw dauncer he wis in his time, thought Ina as she faced her husband, wheelchair-bound in the Tullyburn Residential Home on a summer day in 2009. Now she and Davie could take him only so far as their favourite walk in Letham Glen, as he would become agitated if they ventured to take him further into the woodlands. At the final turn of the trail was the wooden bridge which had featured during their courting days, with a small, papply waterfall just below.

Vwaddie's initial charms had given way, soon after their wedding, to an assertiveness deriving from macho military tradition. Ina's relatives had claimed variously that what could you expect if you married a foreigner, and a Pape forby, or that these folk didnae appreciate what our Russian allies had suffered – this was the time of the 'Poles Go Home' stishie – and there was the lingering native-macho grumbling that these buggers had stolen 'our' womenfolk, of whom Ina was a supreme symbol. In due course, as we know, her man was accepted by his mates doun the pit; and the family had to admit that the pair of them, Ina, ay, and the Vwaddie-craitur, were doing well by oor Davie, who could no doubt be a handful with all his problems and that.

Ina hadn't taken long, in these early days, to show Vwaddie who was the real gaffer in the Makarowski household, i.e. herself. 'See that Ina,' observed her friends. 'She never pits a fuit wrang. Ye dinnae mess wi Fife women.' Such a woman as Ina, though, achieved her results not by physical bulk – which she conspicuously lacked – but (above all) by a certain facial expression. That alone succeeded in getting Vwaddie to moderate his intake of bevvy: she didn't need to verbalise the fact that he wasn't in his barracks now. This phenomenon became known as the Ina

Stare. The Ina Stare could convey many meanings: that she was angry with you but wasn't going to argue with you, just do as she says; that she was awfy fond of ye and there was naething she wouldnae dae for ye, as long as ye behaved yersel; or that she was utterly puzzled, bumbazed, dumbfooonert by the ways of the world and by your contribution – either dubious or benign – to those ways of the world.

That last was the main characteristic of the Ina Stare: behind it, you could tell, she was trying (with some difficulty) to figure it all out.

Almost twenty years earlier than the wheelchair outings from Tullyburn down to Letham Glen, Ina had cause to stare as never before.

During the late 1970s, and into the 1980s and a little beyond, Lady Marion Bruntsfield became first an occasional, then a frequent, visitor to the Makarowskis. She opted to remain Lady Marion Bruntsfield, if only in name, ignoring the 'absurd bluster', as she put it, of her ex-husband Sir Andrew.

The baronet had filed for divorce when he caught her in bed with Scotland's rugger hero, his nephew Rab Bruntsfield. 'Just because Rab's tremendously good in a scrum,' claimed Marion, 'and Andrew isn't.' Gossips delighted in speculating on what she meant by a scrum, and in remarking that she could have continued to call herself Lady Marion Bruntsfield, more or less legitimately, if Rab hadn't gone on to dump her for a much, much younger woman.

Marion found herself reliant on the Makarowskis for company and understanding. As well as at Ina's home, the two women would meet in Leven town centre. Occasionally they would head for the Shoreheid Café for fish and chips, a novel experience for Marion, but more often at Stuart's for tea and shortbread. That latter ambience of feminine gentility was ideal for the mid-way point to which they were travelling from their respective stations in life.

Ina preferred to avoid the Leven pubs which Marion would frequent as additional sources of solace. Their meetings in town became restricted to the centres of fish and chips and tea and shortbread, with now and then strolls along the shores whenever Marion was relatively steady on her feet. Ina was never invited to Marion's small flat in East North Street, and assumed that 'mebbe it wis because it wis a midden'; moreover, Marion refused all her offers of help with her domestic issues. More to the point, Marion's visits to Ina's house ceased.

This happened unexpectedly and abruptly.

One afternoon in 1992 Ina and Marion arrived together at the Makarowski home after a 'jaunt' in town. Davie, who came to the door to meet them, displayed his nervous tics at their most acute. Marion always felt uneasy in his presence; now she experienced a vague alarm.

'Whit's the matter, Davie son?' asked Ina.

Davie stammered: 'Uncle. It's uncle. Don't come in.'

'Calm doun, son. Did ye gie him his pill?'

'It's not that, Auntie. It's –'

Ina gently motioned him aside and entered the living room with her friend. 'Vwaddie, here's Marion, she's an awfy lot better nou – Vwaddie, ye look terrible –' With both difficulty and determination he had risen from his armchair and Ina became suddenly aware that he was pale and trembling.

'*Szanc … Szanc … zdrajca!*'

He was short of breath, but he kept repeating these words. Otherwise shaking, he pointed firmly at Marion.

'*Szanc. Zdrajca, zdrajca.*'

Marion glared at Davie and seemed to panic: 'Why does he repeat my family name?'

Ina's stare conveyed only numbness. She was unable to speak.

'I know no Polish, young man,' said Marion, regaining a little of her sometime poise. 'What is he saying?'

Davie, like his aunt, was in shock.

Władysław Makarowski stumbled towards Marion, who recoiled. 'That woman. She is Szanc. I want her to go. She must never come here again.'

At that Ina found her voice. 'She's my friend, Vwaddie. I'm her friend. She hasnae got onybody –'

'*Szanc*. No good. *Zdrajca*.' He fell back into his chair. Ina could look neither at him, nor at Davie, nor at Marion: she stared ahead, at a framed drawing of the main square in Kraków.

Davie knew that it must be his move:

'*Zdrajca*. It means traitor.'

Szanc … traitor: Marion mechanically took in the combination of these words; her expression was blank. There was silence in the room, apart from Mr Makarowski's muttering in Polish.

Lady Marion Bruntsfield ran from the house. Ina called her back, but she disappeared at the end of the street.

Davie attempted to comfort his aunt:

'What else could I do?'

She accepted his embrace.

'I dinnae blame ye, son. But Ah'm no gonnae desert her.'

Seventeen years later, in the Tullyburn Residential Home, as Ina held the hand of her shrunken husband, her nephew entered the old man's room.

'What's he like, Auntie?'

'No sae good, son, There a wee bit o a smile, though, it comes and goes, like.'

Davie had been approached by the young carer who told him that Mr Makarowski was a lot calmer, that he no longer 'said that funny thing – the one that soundit like "dry it, sir".'

'Yes, that's good,' Davie had absently replied.

Two days later the end came. Ina kissed her Vwaddie on the forehead, followed by Davie. They walked quietly towards town; Tullyburn is situated on the brow of a hill, from which they could regard the higher uplands of Largo Law and the Lomonds, and also look down through a tree-lined fence at Letham Glen. In the summer heat, the coconut-like smell of gorse was at once overpowering and appealing.

In the kirkyard beyond, some way down from the ruin that had served a faith distant from that of the old settler, rose his headstone:

WŁADYSŁAW MAKAROWSKI

BELOVED HUSBAND OF INA AND UNCLE OF DAVID

BORN NOVEMBER 27, 1921, BRYNÓW, KATOWICE, POLAND

DIED JUNE 25, 2009, LEVEN, SCOTLAND

6

STATEMENT OF DR DAVID URE, RESEARCH FELLOW IN HISTORY, UNIVERSITY OF GLASGOW

I am a researcher. I am also a nephew. I realise that my objectivity will be called into question. I am not pedantic, but punctilious. I am concerned with facts. I shall not be their sole interpreter.

I love my aunt. I loved my uncle. He taught me much. He also wished to learn from me. My research has been an academic project. It has also been a family obligation.

Since the fall of Communism in 1989 many documents from the 1940s and beyond have come to light. On the basis of my prior knowledge, and with contacts supplied to me by colleagues at Glasgow and at new research centres in Poland, I was able to discover much of which my uncle had been unaware.

During late May of 1989 I had been in Warsaw on a fairly routine research trip. It concerned nothing controversial. During the last few years of the 1980s, at a time of relative relaxation – relative, that is, to the beginning of the decade with the emergence of Solidarność and General Jaruzelski's imposition of martial law – I had been in the country to resolve for myself a few minor matters of Polish literary history. I would take the opportunity to brave the dilapidated railway system to visit Uncle Władysław's relations in the south. The period between the round-table talks and the Solidarność victory in the first partially-free elections – now, that was altogether different. One day in that spring of '89, I walked up Marszałkowska Street in Warsaw, opposite the Palace of Science and Culture, and noted the booths with Solidarność campaigners. Uniformed men in their high boots passed them by, utterly unconcerned.

Almost exactly three years later I was ready to examine more deeply than ever before the country's history and culture. My period was no longer the post-1863 and positivist climate in literature and the arts, but that through which my uncle had lived. I disembarked from a crowded tram at the stop by the approach walkway to the Biblioteka Narodowa. There I consulted a number of documents which, though uncatalogued, had been made available to me. My findings led to a discussion of my notes with academic colleagues at the University of Warsaw, and I collated their views with the materials to which I had access at the various independent collections of archives.

I was therefore enabled to place my trust in certain individuals in the shadows. I came to understand more and more why so many theatres and art galleries in Poland were named 'Labirynt' (Labyrinth) or presented works with that title. In a cellar on the Praga side I encountered a fellow whose head resembled a large egg and who wore dark glasses even in the dark. 'Kojak' they called him. I was glad that two of my scholarly colleagues had accompanied me down these metal stairs into that dank vault.

We viewed the film which 'Kojak' produced from a safe. He made a copy on VHS tape; after checking it, we handed over the money, and made our exit as discreet as our entry.

Back in Leven, I was ready to play the tape to Uncle Władysław, and thereafter to show him the photocopies of the documents which I had scrutinised in Warsaw. I pressed the button, and he leaned closer to the screen: his cataracts had been troubling him.

The history of the noble and patriotic family of Szanc, to which Lady Marion Bruntsfield was related on her mother's side, had come to an abrupt end as far as its official documentation was concerned. Lady Muriel had never met any of these relations, and her mother had possessed only three photographs of them, all womenfolk.

I must stress that as well as wishing to obtain for my uncle information on his former commanding officer, Major Józef Szanc, I hoped that Lady Muriel, my aunt's unlikely friend, would also take an interest in my findings. She had shown no curiosity whatsoever about my university work and I wished to demonstrate to her that I was by no means a negligible person. To reiterate: I'm concerned with facts, as I see them.

The tape showed a group of Nazi officers approaching the ruins of the Royal Castle in Warsaw. The cameraman was filming from a distance, the images were jerky, and it may be that the footage was clandestine: possibly the officers would have ordered the cameraman to be shot had they been aware of what he was doing. I cannot tell you for sure. However, my uncle, Władysław Makarowski, recognised one of the Nazis and turned pale.

'He laughs … he laughs …'

The Nazi officer was Józef Szanc, the one-time Polish Army major whom Makarowski had venerated. The man was expressing his amusement at the destruction of one of the great symbols of Polish nationhood.

When Władysław Makarowski – my uncle – came out of his dazed condition, he began to weep uncontrollably. Then anger took over.

'*Zdrajca!*'

Lacking support from a patriotic population, Polish collaborators were rare. This was not Vichy France or Norway whose Vidkun Quisling had regarded himself as a guardian of the blue-eyed race. Indeed, Makarowski, who had smiled nervously at the vulgar jokes of his major, including the anti-semitic ones, had learned in Scotland about those many Poles who, risking their lives, had sheltered Jewish families. Prior to his defection, Szanc had a way with his men, his crude drinking-buddy bonhomie creating a macho bond which the more cultivated of his fellow-officers regarded with disdain.

So, fifty years later, and in my presence, my uncle Makarowski – once he had calmed down somewhat – inspected the documents which I had brought from Warsaw. They confirmed (beyond all doubt, let me add) that Józef Szanc had successfully Aryanised himself, almost homophonically, as Josef Schanz. Certainly he had German as well as Polish blood and with his low cunning had convinced the occupying authorities to accept him as one of them, and he was made a colonel.

Why, though, did he not choose another Teutonic name? Surely that would have offered him better cover? Yet they say that all brutes have a sentimental streak, and he may have wished to preserve at least something of his previous identity. The man was an IDIOT.

On both sides – Schanz and his new allegiance – there was wiliness commingled with stupidity, the formula which allowed Nazism to flourish in the first place. Schanz formerly Szanc had read Nietzsche in a half-baked manner and his brain had become drunk on the racial theories of the wretched Alfred Rosenberg. So he was led to betray his original country (the Poles were not 'racially pure', after all) and became useful to his new masters for the information he could furnish them on the Polish forces. His mediocrity was recognised when they gave him a desk-job: doubtless he allowed himself a little smirk at the thought that bureaucrats, being obscure, could escape reprisals in the unlikely event of the defeat of the Reich. When the unlikely event actually occurred, Schanz destroyed all incriminating documentation (or so he thought) and contrived a new life for himself and a favourite mistress in one of the more welcoming Latin American republics. I know not how he fared thereafter: I know no Spanish. In any case, I had accumulated all the information that I required.

Lady Marion Bruntsfield has never recovered from the loss of her family honour, and I'm sorry for what became of her. She is the friend of my Auntie Ina, who does not blame me for the revelations. I am resolved to comfort Uncle Władysław to the best of my ability; it was all a long time ago, and if I am right about one thing it's that he has nothing to be ashamed of. Far from it. He is the bravest and kindest of men, a true son – as Joseph Conrad wrote in 'Prince Roman' – of 'that country which demands to be loved as no other country has ever been loved, with the mournful affection one bears to the unforgotten dead'.

7

In the years immediately following Marion's retreat from her home, Ina's encounters with her friend were accidental and sporadic. She attempted to call on her at her flat in East North Street, contrary to the earlier arrangements between the two women; Marion was either away or was not answering the door. Ina's distress increased, especially when her friend's neighbours advised her not to make further attempts.

'She shuid gang hame,' one said. 'Whaurever she comes frae.' 'Thinks she's better than ordinary folk,' said another. A passing drunk grinned as he stumbled towards Ina: 'Dinnae bother aboot her, hen. She's an auld hüre.'

Ina plucked up courage to enter the town's pubs: Marion had been barred from them all. One young member of the bar staff had taken pity on her, however, and informed Ina that the lady would go 'walkabout'. He had to explain to Ina what that meant.

One day in 1996 Ina saw Marion walking unsteadily along the beach, and feared that her friend might head for the water. She persuaded the outcast to let her guide her to her home. Once inside, Ina was horrified by the mess: the flies gathering on abandoned food; thick dust on the broken furniture and on tilting shelves; broken crockery littering the floor. There was a strong smell of urine. What appeared to be a bed was in such a dishevelled state that Ina was initially reluctant to attempt to tidy it.

Ina realised that she would need help with all this.

Davie's a busy man, I ken, she thought, *but mebbe …*

Her nephew indicated that on his return to Glasgow after a conference, he would take the bus to Leven. Ina met him at the Shoreheid station.

'Ah need ye ti help yer auntie …'

'That's why I'm here, Auntie Ina. I'll aye come when ye want me.'

'Ah dinnae mean me, son. Ah meant yer aunt Marion – ' Ina suddenly realised what she had just said. Davie stared.

'Oh.'

Lady Marion Bruntsfield had retained her title, partly because of her long-lost Rab, but mainly because she had no other 'name'.

There had been a rift with her father's side of the family. Her brother had sold the estate but remained in Surrey as a stockbroker, commuting to the City. Marion would maintain that he and his brood were not on her wavelength; they maintained that she wasn't on theirs. As they lost touch Marion was unable to trace them to claim her share of the family fortune, such as it was or might have been.

So Ina and Davie cleaned and tidied Marion's flat, making it habitable again. Marion stretched out a withered arm towards Davie, who blinked and twitched.

As they returned to the Makarowski home, Ina remarked to her nephew:

'I mynd o somethin yer Uncle Vwaddie yuised ti say afore he stertit ti fail. He wad talk aboot the "Polish tragedy". Ah cuidnae aye follae whit he meant by it, but Ah had a wee bit o an idea.'

'Ay, Auntie,' replied Davie. 'And it was very much his own Polish tragedy.'

'Ay, and hit wis somebody else's.'

'It was a lot of folk's, Auntie. The Polish tragedy.' Ina stared at him quizzically.

'Ah meant it wis Marion's … yer aunt Marion's. Ay, hit wis Marion's Polish tragedy anaa. Ah dinnae ken why folk cannae juist get on wi each ither.'

◎◎◎

A month or so later, Ina and Davie called at Marion's flat but there was no answer. Ina wondered if her friend had gone 'walkabout' again.

They found her slumped on a bench by the Shell House, as if she had made for the beach but could not go any further. The Shell House was so called because an eccentric former occupier had covered it with shells, except for the windows. In the garden, by way of an ornament, was a small bus, also covered with shells except for the windows and the indication of a never-never destination: DUNDEE. The wall against Marion's bench was covered with a mélange of … shells, cheap jewellery, shards of broken pottery and pieces of broken mirrors.

Ina gasped: Marion was thinner and paler than ever.

Davie knelt before the bench, leaned forward, and kissed Marion on her forehead. There was a coldness on his lips: she was dead.

8

'Dr Ure, your aunt was in the grounds but has gone. The gate was open. It hasn't happened before –'

Ina's nephew received the call from Tullyburn Residential Home. Fortunately he was in Leven, putting the house in order in preparation for its imminent vacancy.

'It's all right, I know where she'll be.'

She'd only have gone down the hill and into Letham Glen. She liked to sit in the sunken garden and watch the young mothers with their children at the adjacent playground. Latterly she would just sit and stare.

Davie strode under the arch which forms the entrance to the glen. He looked to his left, towards the sunken garden: she wasn't there. He began to panic.

Oh no – all that traffic –

The main St Andrews – Kirkcaldy road passes in front of Letham Glen. On the other side is the Scoonie kirkyard.

She'll be there, thought Davie, *but the cars would have to screech to a halt for her. She could easily have been knocked down.*

He took the nearest pedestrian crossing and entered the cemetery. He neared the ruined kirk and approached the grave of Władysław Makarowski. The inscription faced the sea. Davie found his aunt crouched before the headstone; she was dropping dried-up flowers on the grave, at which she intently stared. He took her hand and eased her gently to her feet. She mumbled incomprehensibly, as if she had just come out of one of her *dwams*, as she called them.

'Come on, Auntie. Let's get ye to the home.'

'Hame? Hame?' she replied, with a renewed if passing clarity. 'Whaur's my hame?'

The Kilt

THE KILT

Skočna

1

He enjoyed the coastal walk of the Moray Firth, preferring the direction of Cromarty. Twenty years earlier, he would have made it all the way to that town; now he was happy enough, Angus Cooper, to reach the abandoned lighthouse on a large outcrop some ten kilometres north-east of the ancient county town of Inverpeffer.

Angus was born and raised in Dunfermline during the late 1940s and early 1950s; he had spent most of his working life in Edinburgh University Library. Shortly after his retirement he had flitted north with his third wife, whose family belonged to Inverness, or the 'Highland capital' as she called it. The couple settled in a suburb of Inverpeffer and used their bus passes within a fairly limited radius; even a trip to Inverness was a rarity, despite the city's many attractions for Angus.

He made few friends and when he went into town he avoided the pubs. His favourite destination was the sole remaining independent bookshop in Inverpeffer. It was the neighbour of a former Catholic church directly facing the Victorian iron bridge over the River Ross; in the aftermath of the floods of some years back, Angus had felt deprived of his browsings, but the shop miraculously reopened with new arrivals of second-hand stock, mostly ex-library. Angus rarely encountered the owner, who dealt in his office with online orders. Behind the counter there sat a young lady of twenty who served customers, tapped at a keyboard, and from time to time sorted out the shelves.

Angus savoured the melancholy ambience, as he put it, of a repository of discarded pasts.

The girl was a student at the town's Ardairnie College, and in the shop was earning 'a few bawbees', as Angus surmised, to see her through her studies. He knew little about her as they rarely conversed. However, on one particular day during the spring of 2007, she turned from a corner of the shelves and:

'There's a batch of stuff came in this week, Dr Cooper. It might interest you, foreign languages and that. Ardairnie's been doing a clear-out.'

'Thanks.'

Angus knew the background to this hoard. The College had closed its Department of Humanities and was reducing its library's holdings of modern language materials. It was now concentrating on its new Centre for Enterprise, Innovation and Opportunity. The only language which was now being 'developed' was Chinese, and indeed the rising stars of Shanghai's Communist élite were now looking very favourably on Ardairnie.

Angus rummaged among the piles indicated by the girl. Clearly they were not considered to be worth sorting out – he picked up volume 1 only of Balzac's *Illusions perdues* and volume 2 only of the Dostoyevsky novel usually translated as either *The Devils* or *The Possessed*.

There were bundles of *Paris Match* tied up with string. They smelled of damp. The run went back to the 1960s and Angus became increasingly curious as he surreptitiously cut the string with his penknife.

He recalled how *Paris Match* photographers would risk (and, on occasion, lose) their lives in covering world events of the mid- and early-late twentieth century. He felt a rush of excitement when he came to an unbroken run of issues from January through to September 1968. As he was kneeling on the floor he became uncomfortable and decided to carry the magazines to a stool and table by the history section.

He found that he was reliving memories of that year, and above all of the turbulence in Czechoslovakia from the unlikely ascent of a shy, unassuming man – Alexander Dubček, who became viewed as a potential liberator - through to the Prague Spring, the invasion, and its traumatic aftermath. Angus felt his eyes becoming moist, though he dismissed this scornfully as the lachrymosity of a man with a diminishing future.

He took up one of the later issues of the run of *Paris Match*. It contained photographs of young people with expressions of utter despair. The Czech rather than the French word for 'why?' – PROČ? – appeared in large letters above a girl whose face was the very image of beauty and tragedy.

Christ, thought Angus Cooper, *it's Hana.*

The former holdings of Ardairnie College Library extended well into an alcove where a plastic basket contained a jumble of items priced at 25 pence each or £1 for ten. Angus found more items of Czechoslovak interest, including a 'White Book', published in Moscow and in English translation: it was a defence of the invasion. There were a number of plates: one photograph purported to show a rotund West German orator calling for 'revanchist' annexation of the Sudeten territories by the Bonn state; another showed an elderly gentleman indignantly staring at a swastika chalked on a Prague wall, with a caption claiming that fascists had been fuelling the discontents – though the graffiti had likely been put there by a protester to equate the Soviet-led invasion with the Nazi repression three decades earlier.

Then Angus noticed a slightly blurred photograph in which he could recognise one of the streets in the Old Town; the rubric amounted to a dark muttering on the presence of 'foreign agents' during the spring and summer. There was the figure of a pedestrian with a beard and a markedly unCzech garment around his haunches: a kilt.

Christ, thought Angus Cooper, *that's me.*

2

By October of 1967 he was settling into his 'year out' at the Charles University. There had been a gradual and partial relaxation of the system, though he was advised to be on his guard: anything could happen, they said.

For all that, he blundered about somewhat. During the first days in the hostel, unfamiliar with the signage on doors, he entered the women's bathroom area and a girl hastily covered herself with a towel – *'Ce n'est pas pour les hommes!'* OK, he thought, here it's international but not intersexual, and he smiled at his childlike awe in this new old world.

The hostel was known as Větrník and was situated just off the long boulevard running through the western district of Střešovice. At first, unsure of the trams, he would walk all the way, within sight of Hradčany Castle and St Vitus' Cathedral, down towards the bridge that took him across the Vltava to the main university building. A friendly junior lecturer in the English department took him for tea in the room where 'your Scottish poet, Edwin Muir' would write, or simply enjoy the view, during his periods as a visiting professor before '1948, and the beginning of the new order.'

He was also befriended by a group of students in the philosophy department, and their spoken English was as good as that of the admirer of Edwin Muir. He wished he could make similar progress with his Czech, as learning the language was his main reason for being here, as well as acquiring a general grounding in culture, history, and – as far as possible – politics. When the mysteries of the public transport network had been explained to him, he would return to his hostel initially on foot, following the tram route and practising the names of his destination – Větrník, easy enough, but Střešovice … he must conquer this and much else, he pondered, as he subvocalized along the way, hoping a cop wouldn't think he was saying something subversive and confine him in some subterranean nook.

'Stře … Stře … Střešovice?' His entry to the tram was nervous and felt foreboding.

'Prosím.' Thus was he presented, unsmilingly, with his ticket. 'Prosím' was uttered in the same clipped tone to the next passenger, and the next. He took his rattling seat as and when he could obtain one. Clearly outside the university his rapport with his fellow human beings could not be taken for granted.

One of the philosophy students was Hana Jandová, with her black hair cut neatly to the neck, her bright eyes, high cheekbones and mocking smile. He found her livelier and sexier than any girl he'd hung out with back home.

'Angus, my dear. Have you brought your Scottish skirt with you?'

'Oh you mean a kilt. Yes, I brought it. I'm a genuine Scot.' Winnie Ewing had just won Hamilton for the SNP at the recent by-election – he knew this from his friend in the English department, so he was high on being from one small country while residing in another.

'Then you must wear it, Angus.' Those brown eyes of hers were challenging. Very.

'Yeh ... I should.' He didn't tell her that he was cautious about the kilt in case it got him arrested.

'Yes, Angus. Because we' (meaning she) 'need to see your knees. Only then shall we know that you are Scottish and not deceiving us all.'

The kilt was produced, worn, supplied the necessary assurance, and a bed was shared by the two young people. There followed spontaneous seminars on

Scottish and Czech cultures, initially focused on what they might have described as 'relaxed matters'. Angus explained that in Scotland, the verb 'to learn' meant also 'to teach', so that you had a democratic blurring of the roles of instructor and pupil. Hana admitted that she liked that idea in principle, but that he was the authority on his culture, and she on hers: there could never be an absolute and abstract equality, but rather one that was based on difference and mutuality.

'But I am becoming too serious,' laughed Hana. 'At present my philosophical studies must be centred on the kilt; you must impart to me its concepts and the language which supports these concepts, or is it the concepts which support the language – as if the question was whether the purpose of the buckle is dependent on the kilt, or whether the kilt depends on the buckle.'

'Surely the kilt depends on the buckle, or it would fall about my feet?'

'And there,' remarked Hana, in her uniquely deadpan manner, 'we enter a different area, that of aesthetics. Ah, Angus my dear, so much for the dialectics of the kilt!'

'But you asked about language,' he ventured. 'You can say that the kilt, in order to become a garment rather than simply a piece of cloth without an obvious purpose, must depend on its adornment of my backside.

There's a good Scots word for that, the backside – the bahookie!'

'The bah-hoo-kee. What a beautiful word, as beautiful as that which it signifies.' Hana became pensive.

'Yes, it's a word used in the presence of children, in preference to the arse.'

'The ass … yes … your bah-hoo-kee, it is almost a Czech word – see, we could spell it *bahuký*. Unlike you, we would stress the first syllable, you will know that by now. Angus, we shall celebrate you and your *bahuký*. When the changes come, we will rename a street after your beloved hindquarters – *Bahukská* – there you have it – Bahukská Street.'

'When "the changes" come?'

'Yes, Angus, the changes. And they will happen soon, I know it.'

Even when they were together, Angus and Hana shivered in the student residence at Větrník as November advanced. Lighting as well as heating was poor: switches in the corridors and stair wells would flicker on and off, and the chronically clumsy Angus stumbled more than usual, and that was much. Then Hana learned of a planned demonstration to protest at the poor conditions. Accordingly, one evening she and Angus joined a growing number of students in the Little Quarter Square, outside St Nicholas Church. They carried candles as they headed up the steps towards the seat of power in Hradčany Castle. Suddenly, from a dark lane, the police charged, attacking and arresting the students at the head of the procession. Hana grabbed Angus's hand and they took refuge down a winding side-street.

The next day Hana told him: 'It's the beginning. This is more than the issue of heating and lighting.

'Poor Jindřich, our friend, they got him. It is too risky for us to go to the hospital. He is a brave guy.'

When Jindřich Zlatovský eventually appeared, he was bruised about the face and the top of his head. 'He doesn't say much,' commented Hana. 'He never does. He is deep. A student of philosophy but you never know what he is thinking. The beating will have silenced him even more, of course; he is very dazed. But the government is weakening, and the university refused to expel him.

'Old Stalinist Novotný – his days in power are numbered. He is getting desperate. He has been seen in the pubs of the Malá Strana, trying to drink with the working men and show himself as great proletarian hero. He tells them the students are spoilt kids of those in the Party who want him to go. It won't work.

'Stuff is coming out about his high bourgeois habits, he and his son fixing it so they can import cars from the West for their own use, impress the ladies, sell the cars, make a lot of money for themselves.

'Dubček is gaining ground. The question is, if we can trust him – he is another apparatchik – but he and his friends seem determined to break with the past. We wonder how far they will go …'

Two months later, in January 1968, Dubček replaced Novotný as the Party chief, and controls over the press became increasingly relaxed. Western newspapers became available - 'Don't worry, Angus, we shall be sceptical when we read them too, we have learned to read between the lines.' The problems for the new internal publications centred on the availability of paper and concerns that the print runs might not be able to cope with demand. There were long lines at the bookshops. Angus stood loyally with Hana and their friends as they waited for hours. He recalled that one of the first Czech words he had learned from being on the spot, as opposed to learning from a book, was KNIHKUPECTVÍ, meaning bookshop. On the morning after his first night at Větrník, on that long walk to the university and the city centre, he saw a building with that word on its front.

Nobody queues for books back home, he thought. He was becoming aware of the relative limits to intellectual sophistication in the public discourse of Britain in general and of Scotland in particular. The idea of a poetry reading in aid of a political cause! Yes, it could happen 'back home', as during the CND protests and folk events against Polaris (and which, as a teenager, he had attended), but here in Prague it was assumed that the cultural and the political occupied the same space … if uneasily.

Whenever he attempted comparisons, he would accuse himself of advancing towards conclusions that were far-fetched. He resolved to keep quiet about what was happening, or what was not happening, 'back home'. He was here to learn, yes, 'to learn', and not in that added Scottish meaning of 'to teach'.

But he would continue to wear his kilt. It made people smile, and they deserved to smile.

'Angus Cooper.' His friend Jiří Zítek was savouring the name. 'But we are not like our dear Russian buddies, we do not have g in Czech, we have h. So we might say Anhus Kupa – or, better, not have Anhus, but Jan Hus. He was national hero, you have seen his statue in Old Town Square.'

'The Protestant reformer,' ventured Angus.

'Yes, but more than that, or why would Antonín Dvořák, who was good Catholic, compose his *Husitská* – his Hussite overture? That is serious, I should not make joke.'

'I notice that you guys like to be funny and serious at the same time.'

Hana explained that this was because Jiří was a social existentialist. Jiří laughed at the description but confessed that it was so. 'Social existentialism,' he explained, as if parodying an academic lecture, 'it is about each person's necessity to make a choice – analogous to Kierkegaard's leap of faith – as both an individual and as a social being. When we talk of ideology, we may use the term false consciousness. I believe that this is identical with the existentialists' concept of bad faith. You do not have to follow Marx to recognise that we are made by history and that we also make it: the one does not cancel the other. In other words, there is both determinism and free will; again, to go beyond Kierkegaard, it is not a case of either/or.

'Take Jindřich. He made his leap of faith – a courageous one – to be at the head of the demonstration in November. He was both impelled and impelling, but above all he chose to impel.'

Jindřich missed this encomium. He strolled into their university classroom five minutes later, drawing on the stub of a cigarette. He was pale and haggard, and barely tolerated the handshakes and hugs offered by his fellow-students. 'In this great landscape of bullshit, we search for the smallest jewel. We find it to be no more than a gilded turd.'

That was his sole comment.

By March another group of students, from linguistics, felt emboldened to meet Dubček at Party headquarters. They were astonished at his approachability. They challenged him on the slow pace, as they saw it, of reform. They knew he was performing a balancing act between assuring the Soviets of the Czechoslovak government's fraternal commitments, and maintaining the progress which the people clearly desired. The students demanded a guarantee that the gains would not be abandoned under any circumstances, that the hardliners would not crawl back into power.

'It is you who are the guarantee,' said Dubček. 'You, the young people.'

The linguistics students reported that they believed the First Secretary was sincere. Given their academic discipline, they were able to smell out rhetoric, and this was not rhetoric.

A little later Hana remarked to Angus: 'I am not a religious believer, but I have heard that Dubček was married in a church – quite unusual for a Communist at the top. He is old-fashioned and 46, the age of our parents, of the generation which fought against fascism. He was an obscure bureaucrat in Slovakia, and many Czechs regard the Slovaks as – what is your phrase? – village idiots. It is astonishing.'

'Back home,' said Angus, instantly regretting that over-use of 'back home', 'we students are regarded as middle-class dilettantes, merely rebelling against our parents, that there is no political dimension, nothing to do with social justice. The newspapers and broadcasters portray us as over-indulged and engaging in tantrums. We should grow up, get over our Oedipus complex.'

Jiří puffed on his cigarette, took it out of his mouth, and chuckled. 'Ah yes, the Freudian analysis. I believe we should leave Oedipus to the Greeks, though these guys have their new fascist régime and have perhaps enough to deal with at this point in their history. But Freud, yes, yes, he was banned here, we have discussed him with the professors, like us they wanted to see how much they could get away with.'

'What a professor you are yourself, Jiří!' exclaimed Hana.

'We must take account of the irrational in politics,' Jiří went on, as usual when he was well into his stride. 'Freud helps us here. We are all children of the Enlightenment, and as a man of medical science Freud was a child of the Enlightenment, but his thought should alert us that we are doomed if we ignore the irrational, even as we are correct to be suspicious of it. It is not just the Communists, but the left in general – including you guys in the West – who dismiss love of country, of one's own culture, as petty-bourgeois nationalism and as an irrationality leading inevitably to fascism. The working-man 'has no country'? Oh, yes, he does, and if we not only describe him by his class, but define him by his class, we patronise him as a victim, deprive him of his free will. My social existentialism, you see. Ignore the irrational, or the apparent irrational, and you create a vacuum which the fascist demagogues will be only too happy to fill with their poison, and your working-man will drink it.'

Angus could not keep up with this, but felt he should say something even if it wasn't strictly relevant. 'Many of us in the West,' he remarked, 'find Freud inadequate – he reduces everything to sex ...' Hana smiled at him. 'Jung is more visionary. He respects art and its relationship to the collective unconscious, not as mere sublimation of erotic energies. The material of art he sees as akin to the material of dreams, and without the discharge of semen.'

'My dear Jan Hus,' declared Jiří, placing a brotherly arm on Angus's shoulders, 'you also are professor.'

The Prague Spring took hold, and Angus marvelled at the fluent English spoken by his friends and other fellow-students, while he continued to mumble and bumble in a woefully lacerated Czech. Oh God, he thought, I'm just a wee laddie frae Dunfermline, completely out of my depth here. Then he checked himself for succumbing to such a bout of the Scottish cringe.

The May Day celebrations, this year, were more festival than dutiful in character. Angus recalled that, only last autumn, he had wandered into a dimly-lit vestibule in the centre of Prague, and saw there a framed declaration of praise for the most hard-working employees of a city factory. The Stakhanovite earnestness, together with a smell of carbolic soap, reminded him of his markedly un-proletarian boarding-school in a rural backwater of Kinross-shire, where he had been the least posh of its pupils.

Hana took him to the parade. Even as she snuggled into him, he was troubled by his canniness, his easy resort to irony: all this mass emotion, he pondered, I should be on my guard against it, yet it would be churlish not to be other than moved by this enthusiasm. Let meaner spirits prevail 'back home', he concluded, there may never again be such a unity of the individual and the social being, as gabby Jiří would put it.

On the platform Dubček and his colleagues waved to the crowd. Dubček thrust his arms forward, to fold them in a gesture of embrace. Angus saw large tears running down Hana's face, ah! those large eyes so often turned to him in bright adoration … they were eloquent now of greater loves.

'It is socialism with a human face.' Her voice cracked. 'Oh that it may last. Dubček smiles, and it is real.'

Young people from the West came to Prague in increasing numbers. The city was the new focus of secular pilgrimage. The French told of the *événements* in Paris, and how old man De Gaulle was so out of touch. The Americans placed their hopes in Bobby Kennedy, OK he usedta be a sonofabitch but he was gonna kick Nixon's ass in November and we'd be outa Vietnam … the students of West and East regarded each other with puzzlement. The Westerners couldn't figure out all that common cause with the profs, who were the puppets of the system, right? Take over the fuckin campuses! Jiří took one of them aside and drily proposed: 'Look, Marx may have said that philosophers of the past would interpret the world, and the point was to change it, OK, but let us also continue to interpret it.'

Angus witnessed this, and remarked to Hana how the guy then slouched off, taking at least some of his odour with him. Later that day, the same American approached Angus:

Hey man can you tell me where I can git laid?

A few days later, he came again upon Angus in a corridor and his new request sounded even more pleading in its tone:

Hey dude in the skirt can you tell me where I can git stoned?

3

As the summer advanced, Hana told Angus that it was time to escape Prague and for the two of them to visit her family home in Zlonice.

The small town was well to the north-west of the city, and was celebrated for its red-and-white baroque church on a gentle rise, as well as for Dvořák's residence there during his teenage years. It was a venerable place that seemed to welcome youth: hand in hand with Hana, Angus delighted in its small grassy squares, its paths lined with slender trees, and narrow lanes between houses which, if somewhat run-down, suggested intimacy, warm embrace.

Indeed Hana's mother, dumpy and benign, took an obvious pleasure in greeting her daughter's exotic friend. Hana informed Angus that, to please her mother, she would accompany her to Mass: 'You may come too, if you like, and admire the interior of our wonderful place of worship.' Hana seemed to have forgotten her irreligion.

Mrs Jandová was a chance if traumatised survivor of World War II. She knew no English, but Hana's younger brother Pavel was progressing towards his sister's level of competence in the language. The lad was a pianist, and had gained a repertoire of pieces by the Czech composers from Smetana through to Martinů.

'As you are our special guest,' grinned Hana, 'he is going to play you Smetana's *Macbeth and the Witches* and Dvořák's *Scottish Dances*. He is a villain, he wants to make you homesick.'

Pavel performed many more pieces than these; and in Angus's ears there lingered such alternations of the playful and the lyrical that, in long memory, would mingle with his explorations of the serene environs of Zlonice, in the company of his young lady. They took the trails through the woods, Hana clutching his arm at a sudden instance of bird-song, or the slightly distant church bells carrying their melody over the fields, that the sun-dappling of the branches seemed like a ballet of pure light, the Slavonic dances of nature itself.

They made love by a stream – at the burnside, as Angus expressed it, that language might share in their intertwinings. In turn, Hana translated for him a one-liner which she'd seen chalked on a wall at the university: *I would like to increase our population but I have no apartment.*

'Here,' she added, 'is no apartment. Of course, this is not my time for increasing the population.'

'But if it was –'

'Then the child, our child, would inherit two cultures.'

August arrived. On the greens behind the Jandová home, Angus's kilt, duly washed and pegged to the clothes-line, flapped like a banner in the breeze of its hosting.

Simultaneously, at the Slovak town of Čierná nad Tisou near the Soviet Ukrainian border, Dubček's entourage met that of Leonid Brezhnev. The burly and ample-eyebrowed Soviet leader addressed his Czechoslovak counterpart as 'our Sasha', as if he were dealing with a troublesome adolescent relative who might be wheedled out of his unreasonableness, and if not …

At the end of their talks, there was clinking of glasses, presentation of flowers by children wearing red neckerchiefs, and smiles – broad on the face of the political uncle, thin on the face of the political nephew. By the river Tisa, Dubček pointed in the direction of Moscow, in response to a request from the older man, who might have been suffering from a bout of homesickness.

Dubček allowed himself to be grippingly embraced and kissed by Brezhnev, and the photograph appeared in the newspapers of both fraternal nations. In Prague, the taciturn Jindřich Zlatovský, who included French drama among the many subjects of his current study, quoted the title of a play by Jean Giraudoux, *La guerre de Troie n'aura pas lieu*.

Just over twenty days later, the tanks clattered into Czechoslovakia from the Soviet Union, Poland, Bulgaria, East Germany – and even Hungary, which itself had undergone a similar experience twelve years earlier. Dubček and his fellow-reformers were seized and taken to 'an unknown destination', in the phrase of the time.

The troops may have been ordered to show restraint, but many civilians discovered too late that the reality was otherwise. A fifteen-year-old was painting 'Ivan Go Home' on a wall when a machine-gun was pointed at him from an occupying tank; a woman, noticing this, took her baby in her arms and stood by the boy, evidently trusting that the soldier would withhold his fire. With a single blast, he killed all three.

The statue of St Wenceslas, in front of the National Museum, and at the head of the long, sloping street named after him, became a rallying point for the protesters. Young men climbed to the top of the statue and adorned it with Czechoslovak flags. Around the base there accumulated heaps of flowers in memory of those shot or crushed under the tanks. A line of male and female students, tearful and angry, bore a bloodstained flag down the boulevard. In another part of the city, an old woman confronted a young soldier atop his armoured car and shouted: 'Does your mother know that you are murdering innocent people?' This conscript, a peasant lad from far east of Moscow, wept as he tried to explain to the woman that he had been told they were being sent 'to liberate the Czechoslovak people from a fascist tyranny imposed by the imperialists.'

Angus Cooper was making his way from the university through the Old Town, having been instructed by Hana to meet her and their friends at a spot within sight of the Jan Hus memorial. He approached the area with long, quick strides, his kilt incongruously swishing as if there were something to celebrate. It felt light about his person as if, at Zlonice, it had been refreshed and softened in the Czech country air.

He was aware that he was being photographed. The man with the camera retreated, and though Angus felt a faint sense of recognition, it was too late to confirm or deny this. He dimly reckoned that, in agitated moments, we were apt to imagine things. He was in a condition similar to that in which we are dreaming, but are partly awake and know that we are dreaming.

Hana was with their group, but they were part of a larger gathering of young people who were singing the national anthem, *Kde domov můj?* – 'Where is my home?' On seeing Angus, Hana looked at him with what seemed to him a forced levity.

'Jiří is out of tune, as usual,' she smiled, at first meltingly, then wanly. 'Ah, my dear one, I am like a witch in *Macbeth*, and wonder when we two shall meet again.'

'When we three shall meet again,' said Angus. 'That's the quote, three – you, me, Jiří – not two.'

'I am sorry, it is two. You must return to Scotland, Angus.'

Angus, in shock:

'Two – are you and Jiří…?'

Her forced levity: 'No, no, you idiot – you holy fool. Jiří and me? Jiří is our wayward little brother, no more and no less …' From the steps of the monument, Jiří hailed him and pointed to the statue. 'Hello, Jan Hus Kupa – my hero!'

'Hana, you're sidestepping – why must I return to Scotland, while you're here?'

'I must be part of the resistance – for as long as we can resist. As for you, your visa will run out. The occupiers will not renew it. Do you know what that means? I will follow you later, reach the West, if I can …'

There was a catch in her voice. The national anthem reached another crescendo, and for a while they could not hear each other.

She looked up, and the tears fell.

'Proč?' she asked the city before her. 'Proč?' – 'Why?'

Angus had never seen her look so lovely as at that moment. There was a strong presence of the western press, and a photographer from *Paris Match* caught that moment. Abandoning all pretence of journalistic objectivity, he exclaimed: *'C'est un tendresse tragique.'*

When the lovers spoke next, it was as if to ward off extreme distress by taking refuge in an irrelevance.

'Have you seen Jindřich, Angus?' she asked.

'Jindřich? Ah, Jindřich … no, I don't think so?' Angus hadn't seen the dour one during these summer months and had half-forgotten what he looked like.

'I wish he were here,' she continued. 'The great expert on the French. He would help us understand what these guys are saying …'

'I have some French,' Angus offered, then the square filled rapidly with police, soldiers, water-cannon and tear-gas. People dispersed chaotically. Uniformed men placed their hands on the lenses of western cameramen, and some tried to wrench their equipment away. There were scuffles, threats from the journalists that they would contact their embassies. In the mêlée, Angus lost sight of Hana, Jiří and the others: had they taken refuge down the innumerable side-streets of the Old Town, or had they been bundled into waiting vans?

Angus himself dived into a pub and into the toilet of its cellar. When the noise died down, he ventured outside, searched the maze of lanes, then realised the futility of it all. It hit him with inexorable force that he would most likely never see Hana again.

He boarded a dawn train at Hlavní Nadraží, Prague's central station with its decayed Secession interior. At the frontier his luggage was of course thoroughly searched, but he had successfully concealed the photographs of Hana and himself at Zlonice. Beyond the barbed wire, armed guards and Alsatian dogs, his journey took him to Munich. It made sense to stay there overnight, and he conducted the necessary practicalities somehow, hardly aware that he was doing so.

The trick was to keep moving: so he had been told, in essence, at the time of collapse of earlier amours. But that phrase came to him much later, echoing the title of a novel by Janice Galloway.

His pension was near the Englischer Garten, and he strolled up to the circular Greek temple on a knoll, took coffee at the base of the Chinese Tower, where he observed young parents as they, in turn, watched their children playing on the grass. It was early September, and still warm. He felt unable to return to his room, fearing that he would not sleep, and instead headed for a raucous and flatulent beer-hall where he ordered a foaming mug. He left without finishing it.

The next morning he took a tram to the Hauptbahnhof and from there the seemingly interminable train to Ostend.

The trick was to keep moving. At Ostend he had a few hours to put off before the ferry to Dover. He remembered family holidays in the Belgian resort: here there were markers of his childhood and early adolescence. He hadn't shared his parents' taste in entertainment, but the beach had been fun, and there had been a special glow in the town's status as the starting and end point of many vacations.

The trick was to seek distraction: there was a kiosk in the Wapenplein but he avoided the headlines of the foreign press, American and British. He was not yet ready to discover what had been happening in the land which he had left behind. Mindful of the Thomas Mann character who spent much of his time in cafés because he considered them to be 'neutral' spaces,

Angus entered the 'Verhaeren' at the entrance to the *galerij*, and relished again its Flemish maritime charm; what was so 'wrong' about simply being a tourist again? Yet he knew the work of the poet Verhaeren, and its humane vision. He rediscovered Corman's International Bookshop, where in earlier years he had cultivated his precocious intellectuality. He was beginning to feel a little at peace, as if the psychological rebound from devastation was already in process.

It wasn't, and that was horribly clear to him when he disembarked at Dover and headed north. It became impossible for him to ignore the news, although Czechoslovakia was giving way to competing topics: Nixon's troubles, not with his Democratic opponent, but with the independent southerner George Wallace; the Conservatives gaining ground against Harold Wilson's Labour Government; ominous confrontations in Northern Ireland; the horrors of the wars in Vietnam and Biafra. The once-promising year, he was certain, was going to end badly everywhere.

As for the Scotland to which he was returning, it featured not at all, and remained the irrelevant province, 'off the map'. It occurred to Angus that he was no longer wearing his kilt: it was buried deep in his suitcase, exactly where he had placed it after the Czech border guards had inspected its folds with unsmiling bemusement. Indeed, it may have been the baffling nature of the kilt which distracted these functionaries from locating his secreted photographs....

In Edinburgh, the trick established itself as distraction rather than as movement, and he devoted himself to his studies. However, in due course he also began to read whatever he could find on Czechoslovakia since the invasion. The months passed, and he learned of the forced capitulation of Dubček, the decent man in an indecent situation, and his replacement by Gustav Husák, his fellow Slovak and former ally. Dr Husák, a flintily-minded lawyer and bureaucrat, had been victimised by the Stalinists in the early 1950s, but was now content to follow his own authoritarian agenda, tightening the police state apparatus while apparently pursuing a policy of bourgeois-contentment for a tamed populace. Politics dwindled, to be replaced with either threats or bribes. So began the period officially known as 'normalisation'.

On January 16, 1969, four days before the inauguration of Richard M. Nixon as the new US President and future buddy of Leonid I. Brezhnev, a twenty-year-old student immolated himself at the head of Wenceslas Square, near the statue and the National Museum. Angus recalled the name of Jan Palach, though the young man had not been a member of his own 'set'. He wondered if those he had known, above all Hana, might follow Palach's example. At

Edinburgh University, he made enquiries of the few Czechs who had found asylum in Scotland, but they could tell him nothing that he wished to know. He wrote to Hana, both at her student residence in Prague and at the family home in Zlonice. Hana might well have written to him. Either way, the letters did not reach their destination.

4

He qualified.

He remained within the orbit of his profession, and after years of service in the public and university sectors, he lectured widely on library science, and gained a small international reputation in his highly specialised field.

He yearned for more expansive dimensions. He went on to write poetry, and it was published in limited editions which found a correspondingly limited readership. In social situations he became flustered when anyone asked him what he 'did'.

Hana Jandová receded into his distant past, a mist and a myth. Then as a decade looked to be gathering around him, he learned of Charter '77 and the precarious emergence of dissidents whose names appeared in memory, notably Václav Havel, the persecuted dramatist whose work he sought out in print and on stage.

He married three times, and divorced twice, as late youth passed into early middle age and beyond. Outwardly successful, Dr Angus Cooper continued to be troubled by a deep sense of unfulfilment, and tried to convince himself that it was merely the banal 'crisis' common to all at his stage of life. That thought served to amuse him, to convey to him that he should stop taking himself so seriously. Maybe his acquaintances were right when they exhorted him: 'Cheer up, it might never happen.'

As indeed it didn't.

During the summer of 1981 he gave a plenary paper at a conference organised by the Royal Library in Copenhagen. In the course of an interval he made an effort to join in the small talk, then excused himself as soon as he felt it polite to do so. Truancy beckoned.

He wandered through the garden behind the Library, and there the statue of Kierkegaard put him in mind of Jiří Zítek and his 'social existentialism'. A fellow-obsessive, he thought with a smile. In the city's Latin quarter, he visited the student haunts, savoured the mingled scent of cigarette smoke, strong coffee and the yellowing contents of second-hand bookshops. He wished his Danish was as good as his sometime Czech, then remembered that this hadn't been up to much either. At the dockside he saw a ferry bound for Poland – a country then in flux – and he wondered if it might collect his lost lady of old: instantly he dismissed the thought, it was too daft even for him.

Didn't she once call him a 'holy fool'? In Scottish Gaelic, there was such an archetype – the *amadan naomh*. Yes, he must admit to himself that he was an *amadan*, a fool; he was less sure of the *naomh*, the holy bit.

As the 1980s trudged on, Mikhail Gorbachev came to power in the Soviet Union and introduced *glasnost'* and *perestroïka*. Alexander Dubček, the man whom Gorbachev would go on to praise, emerged from the obscurity of his forestry job in Bratislava and was awarded an honorary doctorate by the University of Bologna. He was also interviewed on Hungarian TV, to the annoyance of the régime in Prague. Then, in November 1989, that régime collapsed and Dubček appeared on a balcony with Václav Havel to mark the triumph of the Velvet Revolution.

Angus viewed this with mingled delight and awe on TV at his home in Inverpeffer. He saw Dubček make the familiar gesture of arms outstretched, then folded, in a symbolic embrace of the crowds before him in Wenceslas Square.

The cameras homed in on the people filling the square. Angus noticed a woman in her early to mid forties – his own age – and recognised the eyes that wept and the lips that ... no, no, it couldn't be, but it was; she had survived, was happy, and he was elsewhere.

So he would remain, 'elsewhere', for the immediate future. He could do no more than follow the reports and trust that they were reliable. By 1992 it was clear to him that Czechoslovakia might become two states. The Slovaks, according to what he had heard and read, had long felt patronised by the Czechs: even Masaryk, the respected first President, had apparently disparaged the people to the east. Angus considered this as a Scot who was wary of far-fetched comparisons, but who nevertheless couldn't resist a certain wryness of mood.

On his elevation to the top job twenty-four years earlier, Dubček - so much at home in the relatively modest environment of Bratislava – felt ill at ease in Prague, with its imperial past and still grand official edifices. Though he was a federalist and regretted the impending 'Velvet divorce', it would become a talking point that had he lived another two months, he could have become President of the newly-independent Slovakia.

It was also surmised that Dubček 'knew too much' about the internal betrayals that had aided the invasion and the subsequent 'normalisation'. In September 1992, there occurred a car crash in which he was critically injured. A briefcase in his possession mysteriously disappeared from the vehicle. The following November, Alexander Dubček died in hospital, aged seventy, and Angus found himself wondering who were the real winners and losers of 1968 and 1989.

5

E-MAIL FROM DR HANA JANDOVÁ, MEMBER
OF THE NATIONAL ASSEMBLY, TO DR ANGUS
COOPER, ----, 199-

My dear friend!

*How wonderful that you found me from the internet.
What a diligent researcher you must be. But you may not
know that I was imprisoned for many years and was expelled
from the university. Like the others I could only resume my
studies after the changes. Even if I had not been arrested,
I would not have been able to reach the 'west'. I was at the
heart of the resistance, and by the end of 1969 foreign travel
became impossible for all of us who remained.*

*I became a minister in a centre-left government, then went
into opposition but retained my seat and continue to make
my contribution to public life. If our country's application
is successful, I may attempt to become a candidate for the
parliament in Strasbourg. In 1969, we felt that we were
already rejoining Europe. Do you know what that means?*

*You may remember Jiři – Jiří Zítek? The silly man who
always called you Jan Hus. I do not see him much these days:
he became a full professor at the Charles University, and
now occupies himself with what he likes best, i.e. talking. He
lectures on Gramsci, hegemony, and so on. His students are
bemused but they think he is cool.*

It is strange to recall that Zlatovský was part of our group – Jindřich Zlatovský – you may have heard about him and his disgrace, I don't know. Perhaps you remember that he disappeared during the summer of 1968. Well, he surfaced a year later as one of the most ardent supporters of 'normalisation', and Husák gave him a nice soft job.

Yes, in that bullshit landscape he once talked about, he found his gilded turd. No doubt Jiří, who was once oddly fond of Zlatovský, would argue that many who supported normalisation genuinely believed that they were defending a society based on the principles of interdependence and solidarity, principles which were our own. According to our Professor Zítek, these people were not evil but misguided. I find that too abstract.

After 1989, Zlatovský made his second disappearance, but his activities were discovered in the police files at Bartolomějská Street. It was not a good time to be an informer and he was found at the end of a rope in a forest.

There is a spectrum: at one extreme is Zlatovský, and at the other our national martyr Jan Palach. All that connects them is that they were both students at the Charles University, and contemporaries of ours.

And so, our dear Jan Hus Kupa, that is that. Should you ever come to Prague, please contact me at my office.

    Cordially,
    Hana Jandová, PhDr

6

Angus's first professional travel of the twenty-first century was to Prague; he was a plenary speaker, according to the usual pattern, at a conference at the National Library.

As he neared the end of his address, he noticed Professor Jiří Zítek in the audience. No mistake: it was the sometime pioneer of social existentialism. After the applause, and the flurry of delegates around him, the philosopher approached him, shook his hand. Jiří had preserved his ambivalent good looks, at least for the time being. 'And how is our ancient darling Jan Hus? Who was that Spanish goddess who was asking you all these questions? Is our Jan Hus as innocent as we thought he was?

'Or has he become an old rogue like me?'

Angus attempted to coax him into discussing serious matters, but Jiří persisted in his badinage, only now and then pausing when a darker thought occurred to him. His breath smelled of alcohol.

'I had to come and listen to my dear old Hus. Christ, you've changed, I hardly recognised you.

'Yes, it was not Dante's Paradiso that they sent us to. If they'd allowed me to moulder at the university, I'd have pursued research that was ideologically neutral – bibliographical work, like you, old fellow. The safe stuff, just compiling lists. I was never as brave as our dear beloved Dr Jandová.

'Dr Jandová, the people's champion at the National Assembly. She's the real reason you're here. You canny Scot – is it? Christ, this conference looks like it will be fucking boring. I'll meet you afterwards. Let's get pissed together.' He indicated a point on one of the city maps provided for the delegates. When he stumbled off in the direction of the Spaniard, Angus dropped the map into a waste-paper basket.

Dr Hana Jandová duly received him in her office, in the morning, at the time appointed. She rose from her desk, held out her hand. He embraced her, momentarily.

He was shocked by her appearance. She was wan, drawn, and looked older than he had imagined for her stage in life. But her beauty remained through it all: if anything, it was the stronger for the mature dignity that told of her sufferings, and her determination to overcome them.

Her smile was still familiar to him.

'And how are things for you in England – I am so sorry, in your Scotland?'

Angus shrugged his shoulders, and instantly wished that he had made a more graceful gesture.

'Scotland? It still feels very far from the Continent – '

'The "Continent", Angus?' She challenged him with her habitual expression of light raillery. 'Why do you say the "Continent"? You are part of it.'

Silence.

'I must apologise for being unable to hear your paper. My parliamentary duties are unceasing. In fact, I do not think I will ever be able to retire. I am always, as you say, "committed". I am a socialist of the heart.'

She rearranged the papers on her desk.

He stepped a little closer to her. 'I wrote to you. I don't know if you wrote to me, Hana.' She looked down and picked up a stapler which she placed in a drawer. 'After 1989, I tried to contact you, I had seen you on television, I wrote to Zlonice – '

'Zlonice is no more for us,' she informed him - brusquely, he thought. 'My mother died, and the house … please, I would rather not talk about it. You are not wearing your kilt?'

'I don't wear it now.' He refrained from any levity concerning the kilt's relationship, or lack of it, to his ageing backside. 'However, I know much about your public life. I'm pleased that you are sympathetic to the Greens.'

He remarked on the framed photograph of Václav Havel on her wall; she explained that she wished to keep it there, though he was no longer president.

'But I don't know,' advanced Angus, 'about you … you know, *you*.'

She stared at the window. 'Angus, I have had three husbands. I should perhaps tell you that … no, yes, I will … after our release, there was an affair with Jiří, but of course that led to nothing.

'Angus, I can tell. You have not been happy. Are you without children?'

'Yes.'

'It is the same for me.'

She looked at her watch. 'Angus, we have one more hour. Then a constituent is coming to see me, he is worried about rising prices. I fear that he will also rant to me about foreigners, et cetera, and it will be difficult for me to be polite with him.' Her smile revealed more bitterness, thought Angus, than she probably intended.

She clapped her hands.

'But I have a few nice surprises for you, Angus.'

'Oh?'

From a desk drawer, she produced a CD – 'It is by my little brother Pavel. You know, he teaches at the Conservatoire. It is all Czech music, and - oh! I almost forgot, here is my little book, an introduction in English to the history of our two nations.'

'You've written on Scotl – '

'Our two nations, the Czech and Slovak Republics.' She grinned. 'You may resume your studies here.'

'I apologise for not being able to speak to you in your own language, Hana. The invasion interrupted that part of my education – '

'And interrupted much else.' She paused at that, and

resumed: 'But the best surprise is that we are going, you and me, to the music room – yes, we have a music room here, this is Prague, and Pavel is going to play for us. A private recital, a family recital – '

Down stairs and along corridors of the National Assembly building, they came at last to a larger room with a grand piano and rows of chairs. Pavel rose from the instrument; brother and sister exchanged kisses.

Hana seated herself beside Angus: 'Imagine that we are in Zlonice.' Pavel played two cycles by Janáček, *On an Overgrown Path* and *In the Mist*, and completed the programme with a transcription of the great aria from Act 2 of Smetana's *Dalibor*, coupled with Dvořák's *Berceuse* in G Major.

During the last piece, Hana stroked Angus's fingers. He looked up: as of old, she was gently weeping.

◎◎◎

Beyond Inverpeffer, Angus continued his long walks to the abandoned lighthouse and his outlook to the Moray Firth, pleased that he was still able to push himself to such exercise.

The trick was to keep moving, and allow oneself to be distracted. That was not so possible at the succession of seventieth birthday parties to which he and his wife were invited, and where he was careful to avoid the subject of referenda. One of their hostesses, a lively, talkative woman who was committed to making everyone happy, noticed Angus sitting by himself:

'Angus, dear, you must come and meet Harry Goldie. He's a clever man, like yourself. You'll have much to talk about.' Harry was a Senior Lecturer in Customer Experience at the new Centre in Ardairnie College, which would soon become affixed to the University of the North.

'Harry, meet Angus, Dr Angus I should say. He's lived abroad – where was it, Angus? Hungary, Yugoslavia, Czechoslovakia – no: don't tell me, Angus. Czechoslovakia it was! Trust me to know everything about everybody!'

So the good lady delivered him and continued her circulation. 'Great to meet you, Angus,' puffed Harry. 'Prague, eh? Hope you enjoyed it. Had my stag night there. Went back a lot, then the beer got too dear. These days, I'd go for another place in the Eastern Bloc – the new Prague, they call it but I'm buggered if I can remember its real name. Here Angus, let me get you another.'

Angus was content to let himself get pissed with the genial Harry Goldie, having missed such an opportunity with Jiří Zítek. Then he noticed his wife regarding first her watch, then him.

One evening he climbed the ladder to his attic, and rummaged through a heap of items in a far corner.

He picked out his kilt, which he had not worn for

almost five decades. It smelled musty. Why keep it? Elsewhere in the pile were the *Paris Matches*, from the Inverpeffer bookshop, with Hana's photograph under the word PROČ?, and the Soviet book with himself photographed in a Prague street. Pavel's CD was not there: it was downstairs in his study, and he still listened to it from time to time. He would save that at least.

But he extracted Hana's booklet, with her inscription, and added it to the stuff which he would take to the lighthouse tomorrow, and there strike a match. As he wrapped the kilt round the assembled documents, he contemplated the numerous small countries about which we continued to know nothing.

The Carrying Stream

THE CARRYING STREAM

Dumka

1

Hesitantly, Martin Meikle entered the shopping mall. Instantly, he was confronted by an avenue of hortatory straplines, many beginning with the word 'Because'. He reflected that the muzak, these days, would be considered both naff and cool, so much had extremes met. However, he had long recognised that a certain wetness of feeling coincided with impulses towards violence, and the signs of this were merely more ubiquitous, at present, than ever before.

Even more hesitantly, he approached an escalator to the upper floor, then stopped.

It would have been around here, he concluded.

He was standing on the site of his 1940 birthplace, 25 Seggie Gardens, Partick, Glasgow. *Ay, and some gardens they were tae*, he thought sardonically. He recalled how his childhood bedroom window had looked out on to the Clyde, and with a prospect of cranes, for many of the menfolk in his family had worked in the shipyards.

Folk at the other end of Byres Road, by the campus, had lived differently. Martin was the first member of his family to go to university, as a 'mature student' in his early forties. Mature, indeed, he thought; at that time he'd still had an awfy lot to learn, about life as much as about art. A succession of women came into his remembrance, and he shook his head at the eedjit he'd been.

His mother had been one of the characters of that corner of the Caledonian metropolis, a prodigious bletherer at the steamie; she both exasperated and charmed her fellow womenfolk, Prods, Papes, and Pagans alike. She was herself a Pape, hailing from Kilkenny and born Katy Kiely – 'All the Ks,' as she used to shout when she bustled bustily about.

She was proud, too, of the family she'd married into, although the Meikles weren't of the faith and that had caused problems with the Kielys. 'At least,' she'd protest, 'me fella isn't one o dem Orangemen.' She bred Martin in the precepts of the old country, and her husband, a soft-spoken man who only wanted peace, raised no objection. So, at a tender age, Martin was duly expected to prepare for First Communion.

'But Mammy,' he enquired, 'when Ah go ti confession now, what'll Ah confess?'

'Jus tink o someting, Marty,' she advised. 'It won't take yeh long.'

There were certain family myths that were nurtured (and sometimes initiated) by the lady herself. She exhorted him to remember that, one day, a Meikle born in Seggie Gardens would 'go far'. Martin must have taken this to heart somehow, as he discovered a flair for languages, attracted by the prospect of cultures more polychromatic than any that were discernible in 1950s Partick. He also discovered, however, that there were strict limits to his mother's interpretation of 'going far'. Rummaging through his drawers when he was out with his pals (as he claimed), she found a packet of condoms, and gave the lie to the notion that there is no such thing as an Irish volcano.

A little further into his teens, Martin announced that he was getting good marks for his Spanish, and was going on to learn Portuguese. His Uncle Andy, a miner and veteran of the International Brigade, was not impressed.

'Ay, ye're goin off ti thae fascist countries,' he grunted. 'Why can ye no go ti the East and learn Russian and aa that?'

'Ah'm as much o a socialist as you, Uncle Andy,' protested the lad, 'but there isnae much in the way o the sun oot there.'

'Ach, away ye go. Ye're as bad as yer mither wi her bloody beads.'

'Ah'm no like that, Uncle Andy.'

'Ay, mebbe no. Ah see what yer game is, son. Ye juist want ti fuck aa thae bonny señoreeties.'

That just made Martin defiant. 'So whut if Ah dae?' (He desisted from adding: 'Ah bet *you* did.')

'Ay, son, ye're awfy good ti yersel.'

Martin learned that this was the phrase commonly deployed by folk in Scotland whenever somebody just wanted a bit of pleasure in this life. *Ye're awfy good ti yersel.*

'In any case, Uncle Andy,' he pleaded in mitigation. 'Maybe Ah *will* learn Russian and aa that. When it suits me.'

2

Standing there at the foot of the escalator in the People Make Partick Millenium Mall, Martin was back in the days when his father lost his job as a boilermaker and the family flitted to St Andrews. The old man had an uncle in the building trade, and was taken on. However, it wasn't long before they returned temporarily to the west, for Uncle Andy's funeral. Where Franco's bullets had failed, a carcinoma had succeeded. Towards the end, Andy swore as much as he coughed. Martin knew he would miss the auld cunt, and had to admit he'd enjoyed their sparrings. Andy Meikle had been a brave man who had stood nae shite from fascist bastards, both in Spain and nearer home; if he'd lived in the Eastern bloc he wouldn't have stood any shite from Stalinist bastards either, mebbe. Surely, and in spite of Martin's mother's scoffing, Andy had been a Seggie-born Meikle who had 'gone far'.

Martin finished school in St Andrews and became an apprentice to a baker in town. The vennels and cobbles of the place fascinated him, together with the history – the Castle, the assassination of Cardinal Beaton, the burning of George Wishart (he declined to speak to his mother about all that), the cathedral's destruction which (he assured his mother) was a disaster not only for Catholics, but for all Scots.

He enrolled in university evening classes to perfect his Spanish – and his Portuguese – and he became serious about, ay, one day, venturing into 'Russian and aa that'. In the classrooms his fellow-students were Fife locals and included a number of bright lassies whose acquaintance he was keen to further. He perceived that the rest of the University of St Andrews was given over largely to posh folk from down south and who seemed unaware that they were studying in a town of Fife; and so, to the young Martin, the extra-mural department in St Mary's Place was suggestive of an enclave within an enclave.

Now, approaching his mid-70s, Martin uttered to himself these lines from Tom Scott's *Brand the Builder*:

> Ye cannae blame the young for winnin free [...]
> Especially in touns like this whaur Nature
> Conspires ti throw them inti ilk ither's airms,
> Open-air love-beds there on ilka hand [...]

3

A few shoppers turned to look at the old guy who was gabbling away by the escalator in the People Make Partick Millenium Mall. They noticed that he wasn't holding a mobile, so he obviously wasn't blethering to someone else. Martin suddenly realised that this place wasn't conducive to a spontaneous poetry recital, and made his exit.

Ay, where was he ... St Andrews ... only he wasn't actually there just now, he was in Glasgow. Anyway, that was lucky, the way he'd been taken up by some of the profs who gave lectures in the extra-mural dept. Jimmy Davidson, of zoology, had noticed him out by the Kinkell Braes, gazing at a gull, and decided to chat with this interesting laddie Martin Meikle. Peter Stevenson of geology picked up on his interest in the coast and took him on a guided walk to the Rock and Spindle, that strange outcrop beyond the East Sands. Dafydd Norbury-Jones, Welsh head of the music department, florid-faced and with his incredibly polychromatic bow-tie, heard him singing in the baker's shop and invited him to an audition. Martin's boss observed to him that 'ye've fair impressed auld Leekheid, but Ah hope it's juist yer voice he's efter. And dinnae you be gettin ony daft notions, son. Music's a braw hobby, but juist you stick in here.'

Dinnae you be gettin ony daft notions ... At the time, Martin judged that this phrase belonged to the same collection as *Ye're awfy good ti yersel.*

Norbury-Jones enlisted Martin for a good many university productions, as a chorus member and even on occasions as a soloist. However, he gently explained to him that he wasn't quite up to a professional standard. So the boss was right after all, thought the young Martin, swallowing his disappointment: a hobby it must remain.

'But Martin my boy,' continued old Norbury-Jones, 'you'll derive much pleasure from that resonant bass of yours and impart much pleasure to others. Now, let's try this great Mussorgsky cycle together.' The prodigious Leekheid then seated himself before the piano in his study and explained the pieces to Martin, for they were new to the lad. 'They'll liven you up, my boy!'

They were the *Songs and Dances of Death*.

Galicia held out more immediate prospects, and he set off. His mother pressed upon him that he must visit the cathedral of Santiago de Compostela, and pray for all pilgrims who are unable to travel ('Dat's what Fadder O'Neill told me, Marty.') Her son made the visit.

There he was, in his early twenties, exploring the Celtic north-western corner of the Iberian peninsula; he eagerly underwent the transition from Castilian to the distinct registers of those folk on the edge of Europe. (Surely, he thought, Uncle Andy would have approved of such defiance of Franco's centralism.) He danced to their pipes, learned their songs and their folklore, discovered their poets such as Rosalía de Castro and those many who remained anonymous.

It was there and not in Scotland that he found his own voices, in the language of the Scots. He made over much Galician and Galaico-Portuguese verse into the auld leid; it was accepted and published initially by small magazines in Edinburgh, then he progressed to original poetry. Pamphlets appeared, followed in due course by books.

In his own country which was slowly learning to know itself, he became known as a MAKAR, a maker, the craftsman who constructs a poem as a joiner puts together a table which is not going to collapse in an ignominious heap. This delighted Martin, but as he approached thirty-five, 'nel mezzo del cammin di nostra vita', he wondered if he could also attain (and deserve) the status of BARD, the poet addressing the people of his land, like the great Gaelic prophets of the North. He saw footage of Chilean miners gathering in a community hall for a reading by Pablo Neruda, and wished that such an artist could appear in Scotland, to teach by his example our own poets and their audiences.

As the years passed and Martin fought against disillusionment and cynicism (while aware of the banality of that struggle), he accepted that he and his peers would be read by few. There was consolation, of a sort. He took a First in English and Hispanic Studies at Edinburgh University, and was awarded a PhD for a thesis on Robert Henryson. That medieval makar had been the Abbey schoolmaster in Dunfermline, but supposedly educated people in that town had confronted Martin with 'Robert who?' Martin recalled that his doctoral supervisor had made the eminently sustainable claim that Henryson was the greatest tragic poet between Dante and Shakespeare.

Martin respected and loved his academic mentors first at St Andrews (unofficially) then at Edinburgh, but he would encounter among the faculty those Oxbridge simperers who denied any merit to 'this Scot lit thing'. At a campus gathering where wine was in abundance, and feeling provoked, he lamped one of them.

He would not become a professional singer, neither would he become a tenured academic. He odd-jobbed, received the odd royalty cheque, undertook whatever literary journalism, book-editing and proof-reading was available. He married a fellow-student who was his junior by a decade; as a primary school teacher, she was the breadwinner.

He became a father and, at seventy, a grandfather.

4

Martin departed the People Make Partick Millenium Mall, past a large glossy ad depicting a full shopping basket with the rubric: 'We saved on all them / At PMPMM!'

He noticed that many of the units were empty; only the larger chain-stores remained, and even one or two of them had already gone.

He decided to visit St Andrews, even if it were for the last time.

He looked into what had been the study of Professor Dafydd Norbury-Jones, the renowned Leekheid. The Music Department had been axed back in the early 1980s.

Old Leekheid had assured him that opera wasn't meant for those posh fellows (who resembled him, thought Martin, in appearance if in nothing else). Yes, the price of the tickets, true, but he should ignore the

loud plummy inanities uttered at the bar during the
intervals. Opera was indeed a people's art – didn't he
know that from his time in the Valleys during the early
'50s when he was a Labour councillor (raised eyebrows
from Martin) and a conductor of amateur groups?

Now, the septuagenarian Martin settled in a café
halfway down Market Street; he avoided the pubs,
having been a denizen overmuch in Edinburgh's Rose
Street during his friendships with his fellow-makars; of
that group, he was a rare survivor. In any case, he knew
no-one now in St Andrews, and did not relish solitary
bevvy. As he awaited his coffee, Martin hummed the
Trepak from the *Songs and Dances of Death*. What a
travesty, he accused himself, bi-Gode, when once he
could sing the whole cycle: a bleak work altogether,
down to the bone and up from the soles of the feet.
It was the Russian equivalent of what García Lorca
meant by the Andalusian *duende*.

During October 2014 Martin was at last able to travel
to Russia and Ukraine. More accurately, he dreamed
that he was at last able to travel to Russia and Ukraine,
the two countries which drove Mussorgsky's music,
the latter – consummately – in the Gogol / Hohol-
inspired *Sorochintsy Fair*. Earlier that year, they had
been at war. The dream was so vivid that he had felt
intrusive. Now, in St Andrews, Martin saw before him
the composer's native village of Karevo, east of Pskov.
How miraculously had Mussorgsky transposed this

landscape of lakes, rivers, marshland and primeval forest into music!

The virtual made aural: Martin mused on the interrelationships of the arts. Music was supreme, and here Martin Meikle had not really 'gone far' as his mother would put it. He was a musician *manqué*. He comforted himself with the assurance that he was at least a poet, and surely the sister-art of poetry was music, before it could ever be painting or sculpture. Words, first and foremost, sang; their other functions, while obligatory (they had to communicate, somehow), were subordinate.

In Maxim Gorky's compilation of Fyodor Chaliapin's autobiography, Martin had learned of the singer's unique dedication to his art. That's it, thought Martin, you had to be serious about it, there was no space for dilettante dabbling. Nevertheless Martin spent many hours listening to Chaliapin's interpretation of the title role of *Boris Godunov,* and this influenced his own singing even if he couldn't begin to attempt the merest smitch of its quality.

Chaliapin had worked with Rakhmaninov and they learned much from each other. Rakhmaninov testified to Chaliapin's care not only for his own role in an opera, but for all the elements of the piece: the singer studied thoroughly all the other roles, and 'every note played by the orchestra'. Chaliapin was concerned for the intricate web of the score, and how the parts and the whole were interdependent: that unity of the yet multifarious work of art, its integrative vision.

The poet, the makar, the bard could learn from that example.

A snell breeze down Market Street was discernible even from the snugness of the café. New customers were taking refuge: he remarked that they were coming from the direction of the School of Modern Languages. They spoke in Italian and he understood every word; they were complaining about cuts in university funding and had clearly resorted to the café as a neutral space.

Martin reviewed his knowledge of Mussorgsky the man. The diminutive young ensign officer had been perfumed, dapper, witty, Frenchified in his manner. He spoke with a lisp, and he made elaborate gestures as he sat at a piano to entertain a private audience. Martin imagined that Uncle Andy, who was as socially conservative as his mother with her 'bloody beads', would have dismissed Mussorgsky as 'a wee poof'.

The Russian's fastidiousness made him averse to discussing his relationships with women, though he once confessed – albeit cryptically – to what he considered a sordid affair into which he had 'sunk'. Martin marvelled that the man who had so heart-clutchingly evoked the love of Dmitri and Marina in *Boris*, and of Gritsko and Parasya in *Sorochintsy Fair*, had missed out on sexual passion. How different from me, sighed Martin, inadvertently uttering his words aloud. The Italian women looked at him, baffled.

Mussorgsky had lamented that musicians, unlike writers and painters, never seemed to be concerned with matters beyond their art: they were not men of ideas. However, he would find himself attracted to a movement: cultural nationalism and its attendant discovery of folklore. The imperial courtiers and aristocrats disdained the growing influence of national elements on Russian music, as in the work of Glinka. 'Cabman's music', they called it. Martin recalled auld Leekheid's horror of snobbery.

Folklore meant demons, bogles, warlocks, so familiar to us in Scottish as well as in Russian tradition. This was universal. Mussorgsky's *Night on the Bare Mountain*, especially in its original, 'rougher' version, matched the sensibility of Martin Meikle; after all, he had translated Villon and Baudelaire into Scots, a language perfectly suited to all that was gothically-grotesque, 'eldritch'.

The operas – *The Marriage*, *Salammbô*, *Boris*, *Khovanshchina*, *Sorochintsy Fair* – were left unorchestrated or incomplete, as drink took hold of the composer. Martin saw in his mind's eye Repin's devastating portrait of Mussorgsky in his last years: unkempt, bleary-eyed, the large red nose, the suggestion of mingled stinks. He had just turned forty-two when he died in March 1881; this was two months after the death of Dostoyevsky, whom he had commemorated at the piano.

Martin had found much to guide him in Mussorgsky's letters, where the composer declared that his motto was 'Dare! Ahead towards new shores!'

That was it: Martin was reminded of Browning's lines, in 'Andrea del Sarto', from earlier in the nineteenth century: 'Ah, but a man's reach should exceed his grasp, / Or what's a heaven for?' What a grasp. Martin the poet and linguist was deeply moved by Mussorgsky's account of his innovative arrival at a type of melody based on human speech; this surely underlined that relationship between the two sister-arts.

The Russian had refused to follow whatever was easily accepted, sanitised, the 'carefully measured drops of prettiness'. The expansiveness of the landscape; of the 'soul' of the Russian people, of whom he confessed 'When I sleep I see them, when I eat I think of them, when I drink [!] – I can visualise them, integral, big, unpainted, and without any tinsel'; this would prompt Martin to hear above all, at the close of *Boris Godunov*, the lament for Russia and its folk by the *yurodivy*, the 'holy fool'. That encouraging but also controlling *éminence grise* of Russian music, Balakirev, had pronounced Mussorgsky merely a simple fool, an idiot.

5

Martin headed for the ruins of the cathedral.

He left Market Street for South Street by way of the vennel where one finds a small garden area with benches and, during the Lammas Fair in August, gorgeous colours in the flower-beds. There are a number of gnarled trees which, if the summer heat allows, are still capable of exuding resin, which glistens in the sun.

On South Street, groups of students, coming from the Byre Theatre, passed him by.

Over twenty years earlier, his reading of Ernesto Cardenal's *Homenaje a los indianos americanos* had prompted his paraphrase of one of the poems:

> The blae o the lift is on your brou:
>   The wund is in your braith:
> Dochter or son, a look frae you
>   Wad fair defait my daith.
>
> Though forefowk frae their efterkin
>   Are sindered bi the years,
> Een reflect een – throu a reamin linn
>   That winna byde fir tears.

He found that to be enharmonic with these lines by the Scottish poet and folklorist Hamish Henderson:

'Tomorrow, songs / Will flow free again, and new voices / Be borne on the carrying stream.' Martin pondered the St Andrews luminaries of the past century – the composer Francis George Scott (so Mussorgskian in his range of the uncanny and the lyrical); the poets Edwin and Willa Muir; and of a generation after them and before himself, Tom Scott, with further lines from *Brand the Builder* – which he felt no inhibition from speaking aloud, whatever the reaction from anybody about: 'The sea crines aye awa alang the sands / And tint youth crines wi it, crines awa. / Yonder the rocks' lang fingers harp the tide / As aye they've duin, as aye they ever will'.

He walked further east, continuing to tell over his spontaneous anthology of his compatriots. Hugh MacDiarmid, too, had known this small town and its ancient streets; in his 'Direadh II', a praise-poem to Scotland's natural eminences, he observes that 'there is no higher ground between us here / And the Ural Mountains'.

'Pause, stranger at the porch', exhorted the speaker in George Bruce's 'A Gateway to the Sea – St Andrews'. Yet Martin felt no stranger here: this town had been the site of one of his several homes, the one in which he had opened up to all that was not himself; the one which – as Bruce's poem reminds us – had been known by 'the European Sun'.

Perhaps, though, Martin had been both a stranger and a dweller, wherever he found himself. He stepped beyond the porch of the cathedral and, almost as in prayer, became himself the speaker of the closing lines of Bruce's great work:

> Under the touch the guardian stone remains
> Holding memory, reproving desire, securing hope
> In the stop of water, in the lull of night
> Before dawn kindles a new day.

1

GLOSSARY

A

aa all
aareadies already
aboot about
aff off
afore before
Ah I (**Ah'll** - I'll; **Ah'm** – I'm; etc.)
airm(s) arm(s)
alang along
anaa as well, also
anither another
arenae aren't
auld old
awa away
awfy very; awful
aye always

B

bairns children
bevvy booze
blae blue
bogle(s) scary ghost(s)
braith breath
braw impressive; accomplished; handsome; beautiful
brou brow
bumbazed perplexed
byde remain, stay, linger
bydin waiting

C

cannae can't
couldnae couldn't
craitur creature
crine(s) shrink(s)
cry call

D

dae do
daein doing
daith death
dat's that's (Hiberno-English)
dauncer dancer
deed ay indeed, yes

defait defeat

dem them (Hiberno-English)

dinnae don't

dochter daughter

doobt doubt

doun down

drappin dropping

duin done

dumbfoonert dumbfoundered, flabbergasted

dwam(s) stupor(s); daydream(s); state(s) of hallucination; swoon(s)

E

een eyes

efter after (**took efter** – derived from, as referring to an inherited family characteristic)

efterkin descendants (after-kin)

eldritch weird, uncanny

F

fair greatly (fairly)

fash trouble yourself, worry

fir for

follae follow

forefowk ancestors (fore-folk)

frae from

fuit foot

G

gang go
gannet(s) glutton(s) (refers to the ravenous birds of that name, but here applied to humans)
gie give
gonnae going to
graund grand
guid good

H

hae have
hame home
hasnae hasn't
hen an affectionate term of address to a girl or woman
his-sel himself
hit it (**hit's** – it's)
hoose house
hüre whore
huvnae haven't

I

ilk, ilka each
inti into
isnae isn't
ither(s) other(s)

J

juist just
jynin joining

K

ken know
kent knew

L

lang long
lawdie(s) laddie(s), boy(s)
leddy lady
leddyship ladyship
Leekheid Leekhead (nickname for the Welsh prof.)
lift sky
linn waterfall, pool, river

M

mair more
mairrit on married to
maitters matters
mak make
mebbe maybe, perhaps
midden a place that's in a mess, a shithole
mither mother

morn, the morning; tomorrow
muckle much
mynd (o) remember (mind of)

N

naethin(g) nothing
neb nose
nev-yoo nephew (posh pronunciation)
nou now

O

o of
ony any
onybody anybody
onythin(g) anything
oor our
oot out
ower too (as in 'too much'); over

P

pairty party
pit coal-mine
pit(s) put(s)
poof derogatory term for a homosexual
puir poor

R

reamin foaming
richt right
roond round

S

sae so
Scottish cringe that odd phenomenon of self-loathing, whereby some Scots consider themselves inferior because they are Scottish
shairly surely
shuid should
sindered sundered, separated
soundit sounded
stertit started
stishie uproar, quarrel, fuss

T

thae these
thaim them
the-day today
thon that
throu through
ti to
tink think (Hiberno-English)
tint lost
toun town

U

uni university

W

wadnae wouldn't

warlock(s) man / men in league with the devil; wizard(s); evil magician(s)

weill well

weys ways

whaur where

whaurever wherever

whit what

whut what

wi with

winchin going steady; having a girlfriend or boyfriend; romantically / sexually involved

winna won't

winnin winning

wouldnae wouldn't

wrang wrong

wullnae will not, won't

wund wind

Y

yer your

yersel yourself

yez you (2nd person plural)

yin(s) one(s)

yit yet

youse you (2nd person plural)

yuised used

ABOUT THE AUTHOR

Tom Hubbard is a novelist, poet and former itinerant academic whose second novel, *The Lucky Charm of Major Bessop*, appeared from Grace Note Publications in 2014; readers are still working out the teasing clues in this 'grotesque mystery of Fife'. Tom was the first Librarian of the Scottish Poetry Library and went on to become a visiting university professor in France, Hungary and the USA. From 2000 to 2005 he edited the online Bibliography of Scottish Literature in Translation (BOSLIT); for this he conducted research in many mainland European countries. Between 2013 and 2016 he edited volumes of essays on Baudelaire, Flaubert and Henry James for Grey House of New York, and a three-volume annotated selection of the writings of Andrew Lang for Taylor & Francis. He is currently preparing a third book-length collection of his poems, *The Flechitorium*, which draws on Fife folklore and tradition, as well as a pamphlet (for Tapsalteerie Press) of Scots versions of the work of the Hungarian poet Győző Ferencz, as well as other translations of Hungarian poetry commissioned by Dr Zsuzsanna Varga of Glasgow University. In November 2015 he was elected an Honorary Member of the Széchenyi Academy of Letters and Arts, Budapest.

He lives in his native Kirkcaldy which has never quite succeeded in getting rid of him.